MURDER OF
THE HONEST BROKER

WILLOUGHBY SHARP

(Portrait from the book jacket of *Murder of the Honest Broker*)

MURDER OF
THE HONEST BROKER

WILLOUGHBY SHARP

COACHWHIP PUBLICATIONS
Greenville, Ohio

TO MURIEL

WITH NO MURDER IN MY HEART

First published 1934.
Front cover: Pen © Koosen | Xiaobin Lin

ISBN 1-61646-211-6
ISBN-13 978-1-61646-211-6

CoachwhipBooks.com

CONTENTS

Death's Dilettante, by Curtis Evans 7

1 | The Man Everyone Liked 35
2 | Murder on the Stock Exchange 44
3 | Enter Inspector Bullock 52
4 | A Few More Suspects 61
5 | Find the 'Common Denominator' 72
6 | What the Waiter Heard 80
7 | A Bottle of Brazilian Burnish 88
8 | The Clue of the Red Metal Pencil 98
9 | Hastings Does Some Explaining 109
10 | Troubles of a Speak-easy Proprietor 120
11 | Alarms and Excursions 128
12 | There Are Two Kinds of Poison 135
13 | Wanted: Fifty Thousand Dollars 143
14 | Rifts in the Clouds 150

15 | The Perfect Alibi 162
16 | A Lesson in Geography 171
17 | Uninvited Guests 178
18 | The End of the Trail 186

DEATH'S DILETTANTE

THE DETECTIVE NOVELS OF WILLOUGHBY SHARP

Curtis Evans

DETECTIVE FICTION of the Golden Age (c. 1920 to 1940) is known for the glimpses it affords readers of the rarefied world of leisured wealth. Yet the clever scribblers who produced those charming tales of classical detection during the years between the two world wars typically drew inspiration more from their vivid imaginations than from real life. For most writers of the period (not to mention most readers), the old moneyed and sophisticated Peter Wimseys and Philo Vances, who with such sublime self-confidence exquisitely swanked their well-bred ways though the gilded pages of Golden Age mysteries, were winsome figments of romantic fantasy.

William Willoughby Sharp (1900-1956), however, was an author of Golden Age detective fiction who actually lived the sort of life that Dorothy L. Sayers and S. S. Van Dine wrote about in their books.[1] Although Sharp was born in New York City, at the time of his birth his paternal ancestors had been prominent in Norfolk, Virginia, for a century. His grandfather was a United States Naval

[1] To be sure, after his 1920s detective novels became bestsellers in the United States, S. S. Van Dine (Willard Huntingdon Wright) lived lavishly—so lavishly, indeed, that after the popularity of his novels declined in the 1930s he could not keep up the lifestyle to which he had grown accustomed. See John Loughery, *Alias S. S. Van Dine: The Man Who Created Philo Vance* (New York: Scribner, 1992).

Academy graduate who commanded the Confederate gunboats *Beaufort* and *Neuse* during the Civil War and headed the Confederate Naval Ordnance Department, while his great-grandfather was a Norfolk attorney and the president of the city's Exchange Bank.

In the 1890s William Willoughby Sharp's father moved to New York City, where he worked as a clerk in the office of J. P. Morgan. Starting his own firm on the strength of a loan from J. P. Morgan himself, the senior Sharp became an extremely successful and wealthy stockbroker. He married Dora Adams Hopkins, a "beautiful young widow" of distinguished antecedents originally from Atlanta, and the couple had two children, a son and a daughter. The elder William Willoughby Sharp held his seat on the Stock Exchange for three decades. When in 1926 he was hit and killed by a taxicab as he crossed West Eleventh Street, Greenwich Village, he was returning home to one of those elegant brownstone row houses that so often serve as sites of the complex killings in Philo Vance's refined murder cases.[2]

Giving some idea of the social standing of the elder Willoughby Sharp in New York, his stepdaughter married Gilbert Eliott, a stockbroker and heir presumptive to a baronetcy, while his daughter married Russell Grace D'Oench, the son of Albert Frederic D'Oench and Alice Grace, a daughter of William Russell Grace, the fabulously wealthy former New York mayor and founder of the great chemical conglomerate W. R. Grace and Company. (At his

[2] *Utica Herald Dispatch*, 6 August 1903, 6; *New York Times*, 28 October 1926. William Willoughby Sharp's father, grandfather and great-grandfather all were named William Willoughby Sharp. Sharp gave his own son the traditional family name as well. The male lineage of the Norfolk Sharps is as follows: William Willoughby Sharp I (1801-1871), William W[illougby] Sharp II (1826-1910), William Willoughby Sharp III (1863-1926), William Willoughby Sharp IV (1900-1956), William Willoughby Sharp V (1936-2008). On the Sharp family genealogy see http://familytreemaker.genealogy.com/users/b/r/y/William-Bryson-VA/WEBSITE-0001/UHP-0022.html. Dora Adams Hopkins was the daughter of Flournoy Woodbridge Adams, a member of the Georgia legislature. Her first husband, named for the former vice president of the Confederacy, was Alexander Stephens Livingston. Joseph Gaston Baillie Bulloch, *History and Genealogy of the Habersham Family* (Columbia, S. C.: R. L. Bryan, 1901), 65.

WILLOUGHBY SHARP
Photograph courtesy of the St. Paul's School Archives, Concord, NH

death in 1904 Grace left an estate of $25 million, or over $650 million today.) Their son Russell "Derry" D'Oench married Ellen "Puffin" Gates, who at Vassar was a classmate and friend of Jacqueline Bouvier (the future Jacqueline Kennedy). Their impending nuptials inspired Bouvier to pen a poem about them, the first lines of which run: "Puffin and Derry in wedded bliss soon will be/Vassar will miss her and so will we."[3]

Derry's uncle, the younger Willoughby Sharp, attended St. Paul's School, an elite New Hampshire prep school, where he played football (second string in the Delphian Club) and served as assistant editor on the *Horae Scholasticae*, the oldest literary school or college magazine in continuous publication in the United States. Already displaying a literary bent, Sharp during 1917-18 contributed to the *Horae Scholasticae* poetry of a rather higher order than that which Jacqueline Bouvier later penned in praise of Puffin and Derry. Lines from Sharp's "Changing Colors" suggest his early interest in the maritime world and foreshadow the setting of his first detective novel, *Murder in Bermuda* ("Rosy coral and black rock shells/Lay where the gleaming sun-fish glide/'Mid crimson sea-flowers and violet stones/Where carmine conchs and blue crabs hide/In the depths of the tossing sea"). With the entry of the United States into the Great War, however, martial subjects predictably came to fore in the young man's poetry. Sharp's longest and most impressive poem, "The Soldiers' Mass," evinces awareness on his part of the horrors of war, yet also expresses his faith in the "saving grace" of God. The last of Willoughby Sharp's war poems, "A Nation's Awakening," written in support of direct American intervention into Europe's armed struggle, is a fervent expression of Wilsonian idealism. Sharp denounces Germany, a "vandal" country that holds to "that vile, ruthless maxim—might makes right," for inflicting "Belgium's agony" and "Kultur on the seas"; and he rejoices that at last the "New World has responded

[3] *New York Times*, 28 October 1926, 25 January 2012; Edward Klein, *All Too Human: The Love Story of Jack and Jackie Kennedy* (New York: Pocket Books, 1996), 27.

to the plea/Of justice, freedom and democracy." This final war poem was published in the *Horae Scholasticae* on May 30, 1918, not long before Sharp graduated from St. Paul's School. Upon his graduation, Sharp put his words into action, enlisting in the United States Marine Corps.[4]

In 1919, Sharp, now a nineteen-year-old war veteran, matriculated at Harvard, where for a couple years he studied English literature. During this time he also wrote some crime stories for the pulps. One of Sharp's stories, "Dead Men Tell No Tales: A Story of Circumstantial Evidence," which originally appeared in *Munsey's Magazine* in June 1921, is included with *Murder in Bermuda* (Coachwhip reprint). A dramatic tale of the trial of a pathetic clerk for the murder of his employer, "Dead Men Tell No Tales" dared to suggest to *Munsey's* readers that lady justice can be capricious. Had personal experience of war and its aftermath blunted the youthful idealism that Sharp voiced in his prep school poetry?[5]

After leaving Harvard and returning to New York, Willoughby Sharp for much of the 1920s appears to have lived the more jaded sort of life of the wealthy young man-about-town. An altercation in which Sharp was involved in 1922 at the fashionable Club du Montmartre, an all-night club located at Broadway and Fiftieth Street, gives us an interesting glimpse of his life at this time. With his friends John ("Jack") Boissevain and Louis Bertschmann, Sharp at around three in the morning left a dance at the Hotel Vanderbilt

[4] St. Paul's School *Alumni Horae* 36 (Spring 1956), 69; "Changing Colors," St. Paul's School *Horae Scholasticae* 50 (May 1917), 152; "The Soldiers's Mass," St. Paul's School *Horae Scholasticae* 51 (December 1917), 63; "A Nation's Awakening," St. Paul's School *Horae Scholasticae* 51 (May 1918), 181. Both the *Alumni Horae* and the *Scholasticae Horae* are located in the St. Paul's School Archives, Concord, New Hampshire. My thanks for her assistance to Lisa Laughy, Assistant Librarian, Ohrstrom Library, St. Paul's School.

[5] St. Paul's School *Alumni Horae* 36 (Spring 1956), 69, St. Paul's School Archives, Concord, New Hampshire. *Munsey's Magazine* had a circulation of around 60,000 in the 1920s. On *Munsey's Magazine* see Peter Haining, *The Classic Era of American Pulp Magazines* (London: Prion Books, 2000). My thanks to Bill Pronzini for alerting me to the existence of this early Willoughby Sharp story, written by Sharp when he was only about twenty years old.

to join a supper party being given by Henry Rau at the Montmartre. "A lot of nice people were there, including Prince Engalitcheff," Sharp confided to the *New York Times* reporter who came to interview him at his parents' brownstone to get his side of the story. Unfortunately, when the three chums reached the Montmartre, the doorman denied them admittance, claiming that the club was closed (in fact this was not true, as Rau's party was still ongoing). When the doorman tried to shut the door in their faces, Jack Boissevain inserted his cane between the door and its frame, allowing the determined trio to push through the portal into the entrance hall. The doorman, according to Sharp, responded by punching Boissevain and then punching Sharp, "very hard." "Naturally," declared Sharp to the sympathetic *New York Times* reporter, "we were not looking for any such treatment in a place that caters to ladies and gentlemen, so that we were taken by surprise." Sharp went down on the floor and was held there by the two Montmartre elevator operators while the doorman continued to punch him, giving him a black eye and a bloody nose. Extricating themselves from the affray, the three young men contacted the police, but by the time a sergeant and four policemen had arrived at the scene of the late battle, the doorman had fled the premises. "Propped up in bed . . . with a piece of gauze covering his injured nose but failing to conceal his black eye," Sharp explained that he had been moved to speak out about the incident "not on my own account, but because of the example, and because this is not the first time the same kind of thing has happened there [at the Montmartre]."[6]

Willoughby Sharp seems to have garnered sympathy over the affair at the Club du Montmartre, but he is said to have scandalized his family when he married a divorced former Ziegfeld chorus

[6] "Society Men Beaten in Montmartre Row," *New York Times*, 22 February 1922. Later that year the Club du Montmartre became a favored target of federal prohibition agents. See "Uncle Sam Starts War on Hip Flasks," *New York Times*, 18 August 1922; "Dry Squads Raid Broadway Clubs," *New York Times*, 30 September 1922; "Dry Up Broadway is New Police Order," *New York Times*, 8 December 1922. Montmartre habitué Prince Vladimir Nicholaewitch Engalitcheff (1901-1923) was the son of a Russian vice consul and his Chicago department store heiress wife. He graduated from Brown University

girl, Muriel Manners. Be that as it may, the Sharp-Manners union was a decidedly happy one and the couple eventually had four children, a son and three daughters. Sharp ceased dabbling in pulp fiction and in 1925 became a member of the New York Stock Exchange, courtesy of his father, who gifted him with a seat on the Exchange on the occasion of his twenty-fifth birthday. In 1928, two years after the death of his father, Sharp with Dudley Harde and Dudley Brown Harde established the rather forbiddingly named brokerage firm Harde & Sharp. The Sharps resided in a Park Avenue apartment with a bar that, most conveniently in the era of prohibition, could be folded back into and out of a wall. Painted with lions and tigers (though no bears), it was known as the Circus Bar. Here Willoughby and Muriel kept what their son described as "a kind of open house," entertaining "their friends and friends of friends and friends of friends of friends."[7]

Of course the great party was destined to come to a halt with the stock market crash. Sharp's son recalled that his father mordantly told him concerning this period in history that upon leaving his office at One Wall Street he always would look "up over his shoulder . . . in fear of being hit by people who jumped to their

in 1922 and joined a brokerage firm in New York. The next year he died very suddenly and unexpectedly in New York at his luxurious twelve-room Fifth Avenue apartment, supposedly of heart failure. F. Scott and Zelda Fitzgerald met the Prince in 1921. "We came to New York and rented a house when we were tight," reminisced Zelda to Scott in a rambling 1930 letter. "There was Val Engelicheff [sic] and Ted Paramour and dinner with Bunny [Edmund Wilson] in Washington Square and pills and Doctor Lackin and we had a violent quarrel on the train going back, I don't remember why." Jackson R. Bryer and Cathy W. Barks, *Dear Scott, Dearest Zelda: The Love Letters of F. Scott and Zelda Fitzgerald* (New York: St. Martin's, 2002), 67. F. Scott Fitzgerald partly based the character Prince Val Rostoff in his 1925 short story "Love in the Night" on Vladimir Engalitcheff. Robert L. Gale, *An F. Scott Fitzgerald Encyclopedia* (Westport, CT and London: Greenwood Press, 1998), 363. My thanks to Helen Szamuelly for helping me disentangle the various incorrect spellings of Engalitcheff.

[7] Linda Montano, "Interview with Willoughby Sharp," *Performance Artists Talking in the Eighties* (Los Angeles and London: University of California Press, 2000), 307; *New York Times*, 29 September 1922, 2 December 1934, 25 January 1936. The daughter of a wealthy Broadway play producer, Muriel

death from the building." In 1931, "not liking the outlook on Wall Street," Sharp sold his seat on the Stock Exchange and moved with his family to the island of Bermuda, marking a new direction in his life. There the family lived off judicious sales of costly pieces of jewelry that Willoughby Sharp had bought his wife back in the 1920s. After a couple years in Bermuda, Sharp felt inspired to compose his first detective novel, in which he imagined murder taking place on the peaceful island. Predictably enough, he titled the novel *Murder in Bermuda* (1933). Sharp wrote his second mystery, *Murder of the Honest Broker* (1934), in Bermuda as well, but during the summer of 1934 he went over the proofs while staying at New York's Calumet Club. Later that year, after the publication of *Murder of the Honest Broker* in August, the entire Sharp family returned to New York to stay and Sharp entered into a publishing partnership with a fellow New Yorker, Claude Kendall, the man who had published his two detective novels.[8]

Although forgotten today, the publishing firm *Claude Kendall* was a quite interesting business venture that sprang up and managed to thrive for a time amidst the onset and prolonged duration of the Great Depression. Older than Sharp by a decade, Claude Kendall, the man behind the company, was born in 1890 in the small city of Watertown, located in northwestern New York, near Lake Ontario. His father, Martin Kendall, was employed by the

Manners claimed to be a descendant, though her mother, of the mid-nineteenth-century actress, poet and essayist Adah Isaacs Menken (1835-1868), but this is a problematic claim, Menken's sons having died in infancy. Of mixed race parentage, Menken, who was probably originally named Adah Bertha Theodore, as a celebrated actress came to know many of the literary luminaries of her age, including Charles Dickens, Charles Swinburne, Alexandre Dumas and Walt Whitman. *Infelicia*, her sole book of poetry, published shortly after her death, was dedicated by her to Dickens. Possibly Muriel Manners, whose mother was Janet (Menken) MacMahon Manners, was descended from the family of Alexander Isaac Menken, a Jewish musician who was the first husband of Adah Bertha Theodore. See Michael Foster and Barbara Foster, *A Dangerous Woman: The Lives, Loves and Scandals of Adah Isaacs Menken, 1835-1868, America's Original Superstar* (Guilford, CT: Lyons Press, 2011).

[8] Montano, "Interview," 308; *New York Times Book Review*, 2 December 1934.

H. H. Babcock Company, one of the largest carriage manufacturers in the United States. The young Claude was considered a live spark, working as a "carrier boy" (i.e., paperboy) from the age of ten and serving on the student council at Watertown High School. At his high school graduation ceremony he was the student chosen to recite Abraham Lincoln's Gettysburg Address.[9]

Claude Kendall began life in modest circumstances in a rather out-of-the-way corner of the world, but he soon moved on to much bigger things in life. His ticket out of Watertown came when, after briefly working as a stenographer in a hardware company, he landed an administrative position at the Mount Washington Hotel, one of great turn-of-the-century grand resort hotels, located in the White Mountains at Bretton Woods, New Hampshire (in 1944 the hotel famously was the site of the Bretton Woods Conference, which established the International Monetary Fund). There Kendall met investment banker M. H. Rice, who hired Kendall as his personal secretary and took him to Europe for four months. After the pair returned to the United States, Kendall settled in New York City, where he was employed by Charles R. White & Co., an investment banking firm, and for two years attended New York University. When the United States entered World War One, Kendall enlisted in the navy and was commissioned an ensign. After the war he joined the United States Shipping Board as a supercargo officer, in which capacity he traveled to both Europe and East Asia. He then was hired by Standard Oil Company and spent five months representing the company's interests in Tampico, Mexico. After this latest foray into foreign fields he was hired as a staff correspondent by the United Press and assigned to South America. Finally returning to New York in the late 1920s, Kendall charted an entirely new career course by founding his own publishing house in 1929.[10]

[9] *Watertown Daily Times*, 24 May 1907, 26 November 1937. The articles from the *Watertown Daily Times* cited in this essay come from the Claude Kendall clippings file made available to me by Lisa M. Carr, librarian of the *Watertown Daily Times*.

[10] *Watertown Daily Times*, 26 November 1937.

The first publication of Claude Kendall was *Uncle Sham*, a controversial critique of American culture by an Indian national, K. L. Gauba, who had been greatly incensed over the publication a couple years earlier of *Mother India*, a book by an American author, Katherine Mayo, which was scathingly critical of India's culture, particularly on account of the treatment of Indian women. The nettled Gauba responded in kind about the United States, often in frank and indelicate language, provoking the United States Customs Service to confiscate review copies of the book that had been sent from India to the United States, on the grounds that the writing was obscene. Having a keen nose for controversy, Kendall successfully published the book in the United States, putting his nascent company on the publishing map with a fine flush of notoriety. *Uncle Sham*'s dust jacket blurb boasted that Gauba's book revealed the "pools of nastiness, obscenity and vice" underlying "the smug morality of the United States." Curious readers—many of whom likely had never even stuck their toes in the water, so to speak—wanted at least to glimpse these pools. *Uncle Sham* sold well, quickly going through several printings.[11] Not for nothing was Kendall using this advertising motto on the *Uncle Sham* dust jacket:

Claude Kendall
Books That Sell

[11] *Foreign Affairs* 8 (October 1929) (review of *Uncle Sham* by William L. Langer), at http://www.foreignaffairs.com/articles/80378/kanhaya-lal-gauba/uncle-sham; *The Pittsburgh Press*, 3 August 1929, 6 (reprint of Lowell Mellett editorial against the proscription of *Uncle Sham*); K. L. Gauba, *Friends and Foes: An Autobiography* (New Delhi: Indian Book Company, 1974), 87. In her introduction to the 2000 University of Michigan Press edition of *Mother India*, Professor Mrinalini Sinha calls *Uncle Sham* "the most famous . . . of nationalist responses to *Mother India*" (p. 54). Claude Kendall quickly followed *Uncle Sham* with a second opportunistic publication of a work making a riposte to a notorious book of moment: Henry von Rhau's *The Hell of Loneliness*, an "impudent and delightfully scampish" parody of Radclyffe Hall's landmark 1928 lesbian novel (then banned in England), *The Well of Loneliness*.

Over the next few years, Kendall published a succession of what often were termed "spicy" or risqué books, attractively bound, printed and, frequently, illustrated. The most notorious and the most successful of these works were four novels by Tiffany Ellsworth Thayer ("Tiffany Thayer"). With several hundred thousand copies sold during the early 1930s, the Tiffany Thayer novels, particularly *Thirteen Men* (1930) and *Thirteen Women* (1932), earned Claude Kendall a great deal of publicity. Other controversial books from the early 1930s that bore the Kendall name include: the first American edition of Octave Mirbeau's *The Torture Garden*, a primary text of the Decadent Movement originally published in France in 1899; *Mademoiselle de Maupin*, an American edition of Théophile Gautier's gender-bending 1835 novel about a real-life infamous French female cross-dresser; G. Sheila Donisthorpe's *Loveliest of Friends*, a novel dealing with lesbianism; Cecil De Lenoir's *The Hundredth Man: Confessions of a Drug Addict*; Beth Brown's *Man and Wife,* about prostitution and the divorce racket; Lionel Houser's *Lake of Fire*, fairly described as a "bizarre tale of identity theft, mutilation, lust and murder, provocatively illustrated with strikingly explicit woodcuts"; and, last but certainly not least, Frank Walford's *Twisted Clay*, a lurid tale about a psychopathic, patricidal lesbian serial killer that was banned by government authorities in both Canada and Australia. Kendall also unsuccessfully attempted to secure the American publication rights for James Joyce's *Ulysses*, which had been banned in the United States on obscenity grounds since 1920.[12]

12 "She loved . . . and killed . . . both men and women," promised *Twisted Clay*'s salacious dust jacket blurb. With *Twisted Clay* comprising a trifecta of casualties of moral outrage were Thayer's *Thirteen Men* and Donisthorpe's *Loveliest of Friends*, both of which also were banned in Canada. *Vancouver Sun*, 23 January 1932, 3. On Houser's *Lake of Fire*, see the summary found at *Golden Gate Mysteries: A Bibliography of Crime Fiction Set in the San Francisco Bay Area*, at http://bancroft.berkeley.edu/sfmystery/summaries/houslake.html. Sylvia Beach, the publisher in France of *Ulysses*, demanded from Kendall $25,000 for the novel's American publication rights, a figure that Kendall termed "absurd." Kendall doubted he could recoup the cost of both a $25,000 payment to Beach and litigation over the novel in American

Like its star author Tiffany Thayer, whose books F. Scott Fitzgerald—no Puritan he—disparaged as "slime . . . in the drugstore libraries," the firm of Claude Kendall developed *something of a reputation*. Newspaper notices that Claude Kendall books received in the 1930s often emphasized what was viewed as decidedly racy subject matter. Middle American reviewers seem to have been especially scandalized. One such individual in Greensburg, Indiana, (population under 6000 in 1930) deemed Thayer's *Thirteen Men* "morbid" and complained that "not even the Russians could pack more unhappiness in a single volume." In Salt Lake City, a reviewer for the *Deseret News* observed sardonically that Roswell Williams' *The Loves of Lo Foh* "will never be discussed at a ladies literary tea" and was "hardly suitable for the entertainment or education of budding youth." An especially incensed Midwestern reviewer for the Lawrence, Kansas *Journal-World* huffed that Tiffany Thayer's *An American Girl* was "an obscene novel without any merit whatever" and that Beth Brown's *Man and Wife* was "a worthless novel without any point or reason." For his part, Walter Stanley Campbell—a University of Oklahoma English professor who was Oklahoma's first Rhodes scholar and, under the pseudonym Stanley Vestal, a prolific author of books and articles on the old West (he even published a mystery, *The Wine Room Murder*, in 1935)—in the Oklahoma City *Daily Oklahoman* wrote sourly of Alan Lampe's *A Torch to Burn* (1935) that it was "another of the spicy novels for which the firm [Claude Kendall] is known. . . . of course the adventures are sad, gay and mad. Those who find night-clubs exciting will probably like this book." Similarly, Kenneth C. Kaufman—editor of the literary page of the *Daily Oklahoman*, a

courts. See Catherine Turner, *Marketing Modernism between the Two World Wars* (Amherst: University of Massachusetts Press, 2003), 193-193 and Keri Walsh, ed., *The Letters of Sylvia Beach* (New York: Columbia University Press, 2011), 136. In his book *Trial and Error: A Key to the Secret of Writing and Selling* (New York: Carlyle House, 1933), pulp writer Jack Woodford expressed amazement that Claude Kendall was able to publish its "splendid" edition of Mirbeau's *Torture Garden*: "I don't see how it would be possible to write a more 'dangerous' book (from the standpoint of the censor) yet it was published."

professor in the University of Oklahoma foreign languages department and mentor of Oklahoma detective novelist Todd Downing—primly noted that the protagonist of Frank Walford's *Twisted Clay* was "a young girl, a homosexual, who . . . indulges in all sorts of sexual experiments, of which the less said the better. . . . it just happens that I am not interested in sexual abnormalities."[13]

On the other hand, some reviewers savored the spice in Claude Kendall books. The esteemed California novelist Gertrude Atherton said of Lionel Houser's *Lake of Fire*, for example, that it had "excellence, brilliance, distinction, originality and high imaginative fire." In his syndicated "A Book a Day" column, the future Pulitzer Prize winning narrative historian Bruce Catton deemed *Twisted Clay* "a creepy tale about the collapse of a mind" that was certain "to make you shudder," while a reviewer for the *New York Daily Mirror* proclaimed the novel "a prose nightmare, tinged with Poe

13 F. Scott Fitzgerald, *The Crack-Up* (1945; rpnt, New York: New Directions, 1993), 78; *Greensburg Daily Review*, 6 June 1930, 24; *Salt Lake City Deseret News*, 27 June 1936, 6; *Lawrence Journal-World*, 10 June 1933, 5; *Oklahoma City Daily Oklahoman*, 22 July 1934, 45, 23 June 1935, 49. Kenneth Kaufman allowed, however, that sexual abnormalities "may, with proper handling, become legitimate material for a work of art." Like Kenneth Kaufman, Todd Downing taught in the OU foreign languages department. For more on Todd Downing and his OU colleagues, see Curtis Evans, *Clues and Corpses: The Detective Fiction and Mystery Criticism of Todd Downing* (Greenville, OH: Coachwhip, 2013). F. Scott Fitzgerald's scornful reference to Thayer appeared in his 1936 "Crack-Up" essays, when Fitzgerald was at a personal low point and must have found the slick success of someone like Thayer especially disheartening. "I saw that the novel, which at my maturity was the strongest and supplest medium for conveying thought and emotion from one human being to another, was becoming subordinated to a mechanical and communal art that...was capable of reflecting only the tritest thought, the most obvious emotion," Fitzgerald bitterly reflected of literary culture in the 1930s. Fitzgerald, *Crack-Up*, 78. The writer Dorothy Parker concurred in Fitzgerald's dismissive assessment of Thayer, writing satirically in her 1933 New Yorker review of Thayer's *An American Girl*: "[Tiffany Thayer] is beyond question a writer of power; and his power lies in his ability to make sex so thoroughly, graphically, and aggressively unattractive that one is fairly shaken to ponder how little one has been missing." Bendan Gill, ed., *The Portable Dorothy Parker* (1944; rev. ed., New York, Penguin Books, 1976), 549.

and Baudelaire substance." A reviewer for the *Providence Journal* deemed *Thirteen Men* "a masterpiece of our time."[14]

For his part, Claude Kendall remained cheerfully sanguine about the stones hostile critics cast at the books his firm published. Of the Kendall novel *Tangled Wives* (written by divorced journalist Peggy Shane), for example, Kendall bluntly pronounced: "It is not the great American novel; it is, however, swell entertainment." In those rental libraries dotting America that F. Scott Fitzgerald so witheringly disparaged, people crowded to borrow Claude Kendall books. With all the money rolling into the Claude Kendall coffers, the publisher was able to take up residence in a luxurious Manhattan penthouse apartment—one formerly occupied, newspapers were wont to note, by the actress Ethel Barrymore.[15]

In comparison with Claude Kendall's more risqué and attention-grabbing mainstream books, the detective and mystery fiction that the firm published offered subtler attractions. Besides the detective novels of Willoughby Sharp, books on the Claude Kendall mystery list included Andrew Soutar's *Secret Ways*, J. R. Wilmot's *Death in the Theater*, David Whitelaw's *Murder Calling* and Willam Sutherland's *Death Rides the Air Line*. All these titles seem originally to have appeared in England and were published by Claude Kendall in the fall and winter of 1934. All are competent pieces of mystery fiction, though only the Sutherland novel, with its unique plot structure and somewhat unsavory subject matter, departs from traditional Golden Age mystery norms.[16]

[14] *Berkeley Daily Gazette*, 15 April 1933, 4; *Spartanburg Herald*, 22 June 1934, 4. See also the review blurbs found on the dust jackets of the Claude Kendall editions of *Death Rides the Air Line* and *Murder Calling*.

[15] *Milwaukee Journal*, 19 November 1932, 4; *Watertown Daily Times*, 27 December 1932.

[16] William Sutherland's previous detective novel, *Behind the Head-lines* (1933), was published in England but not the United States. The name was the pseudonym of John Murray Cooper, who may have been the John Murray Cooper (1908-1991) who was an American war correspondent during World War Two. "William Sutherland" also published in England a third detective novel, *The Proverbial Murder Case* (1935). My thanks for this information go to Alexander Inglis and Douglas G. Greene.

Willoughby Sharp did not formally enter into Claude Kendall & Willoughby Sharp, Inc., his publishing partnership with Claude Kendall, until November 1934, yet he likely influenced Kendall's selection of mystery titles during the latter half of that year. Additionally, Sharp was scheduled to publish with Kendall & Sharp a third detective novel, *The Mystery of the Multiplying Mules*, in 1935. However, this novel never appeared, nor does Kendall & Sharp seem to have published any additional true mysteries over the scant sixteen months of its existence, despite the company's intriguing announcement in March 1936 that it was planning a monthly series of detective novels, to be released under a new imprint, the Clue Chasers Club, presumably under Sharp's supervision.[17]

In point of fact, Sharp apparently sundered his relationship with Kendall & Sharp mere weeks after the March 1936 announcement about the formation of the Clue Chasers Club; and the company, now styled Claude Kendall, Inc., went bankrupt before the end of the year. This was a bad blow for Kendall, but he stayed on his feet and accepted a position with the publisher James T. White

17 *New York Times Book Review*, 22 November, 2 December 1934. A possible exception to this generalization might be *The Second Mrs. Lynton* (1935), a tale by Wilson Collison (1893-1941), a prolific writer of novels, plays and film scripts, yet the book seems to be more a romantic melodrama than a true detective novel. "It is fairly apparent that the guilt for Dexter's unmourned death rests upon either Carla or Beth, her hysterical stepdaughter," pronounced the reviewer of the book in the *New York Times Book Review*, "and it does not require any very brilliant deduction feats for Channing to conclusively prove and correctly pick which lady actually fired the fatal shot." *New York Times Book Review*, 28 July 1935. In the publisher's blurb Kendall & Sharp avowed that *The Second Mrs. Lynton* "is a love story, not a mystery, yet it combines the elements of both types of novels." The Clue Chasers Club recalls Doubleday, Doran's highly successful Crime Club imprint. Another small publisher, Hillman-Curl, launched a "Clue Club" in 1937. See Bill Pronzini, "Hillman-Curl [1936-1939]," in William F. Deeck, ed., *Murder at 3 Cents a Day: An Annotated Crime Fiction Bibliography of the Lending Library Publishers, 1936 to 1937*, at http://www.lendinglibmystery.com/HCurl/Covers.html.

& Co. Sadly, however, the ex-publisher was not destined to long survive his defunct business.[18]

By 1937, Claude Kendall had vacated the Manhattan penthouse apartment once occupied by Ethel Barrymore and moved into a $7-a-week room at the Madison Hotel, located at 21 East Twenty-Seventh Street, just off Madison Avenue. On the morning of November 25, 1937, a hotel maid entering Kendall's room found the ex-publisher dead on the floor, a bed sheet wrapped around his neck. The medical examiner's report concluded that Kendall had been the victim of a "homicidal assault," dying from "shock and hemorrhages caused by repeated blows on the face and neck." Kendall's killer almost certainly was a "slightly built youthful white man" whom Kendall took up to his room at about 3:30 in the morning on Thanksgiving Day. Richard Barry, a fiction writer who with his wife resided in the room directly above Kendall, told police that beginning around 4:30 a.m. he and his wife had heard loud "thumping noises" in Kendall's room. These noises continued for half an hour.[19]

[18] *FOB: Firms out of Business*, Harry Ransom Center, The University of Texas at Austin, at http://norman.hrc.utexas.edu/Watch/fob_search_results_next.cfm?FOBFirmName=C&FOBNote=&locSTARTROW=101; *New York Times Book Review*, 1, 22 March 1936; *Watertown Daily Times*, 26 November 1937. The announcement that Claude Kendall was forming "a publishing firm to be known as Claude Kendall, Inc." was made in the *New York Times Book Review* on March 22, 1936. That month the Kendall & Sharp offices were relinquished and Kendall hired a new editor-in-chief, Geoffrey Marks, a graduate of Trinity College, Oxford, as well as a new agency to handle advertising. *New York Times Book Review*, 20, 22, 30 March 1936. Many years later Willoughby Sharp's son stated in an interview that "Kendall absconded with hundreds of thousands of dollars," causing Kendall & Sharp to go under, but this claim does not seem in accord with the information reported in the *New York Times*, or the fact that Kendall was living in New York, reputably employed, a year later and apparently on decent terms with Sharp. However, it does seem quite possible that Kendall lived over lavishly off the firm's profits, alienating his new partner. Montano, "Interview," 308.

[19] *New York Times*, 26, 27 November 1937; *Reading Eagle*, 27 November 1937, 2, *Watertown Daily Times*, 26 November 1937. Richard Barry, the fiction writer who lived above Kendall and heard those suggestive early morning thumps, probably is the Richard Barry who wrote the lost race novel *Fruit of the Desert* (1920), as well as several adventure serials for the pulp magazine *Argosy*.

Despite having this clearly marked trail to follow, the police apparently failed to find Kendall's killer. Of course, in the stereotypical 1930s detective novel, Kendall's murder would have been solved not by some invariably bumbling police inspector but rather by the murder victim's dapper, sophisticated and oh-so wealthy dilettante friend, Willoughby Sharp (the man even came supplied with a simply smashin' amateur gentleman detective moniker, don't you know). And, to be sure, when he was interviewed by the press, Sharp did have some advice to offer investigators. The detective novelist opined that the murder "undoubtedly" was the result of a robbery committed by the slim young man who accompanied Kendall back to his hotel room; and he suggested that to find this man the police should make "a close check of the bars Claude frequented." Sharp explained that his ex-partner "was a gregarious person, liked to talk, and he was friendly and could make acquaintances easily."[20]

Willoughby Sharp may have missed his chance to solve a real-life mystery (a fictionalized version of the Claude Kendall case might well have been called *Murder of My Ex-Partner*), yet with *Murder in Bermuda* and *Murder of the Honest Broker* Sharp gifted fans of classical mystery fiction with two top-drawer 1930s mysteries, both delightful examples of the Golden Age puzzle-oriented detective novel. The two appealing tales also were excellent sellers for Claude Kendall, and were published not just in the United States but also in England and Germany—though there was a financial hitch with Germany in 1935, when Nazi authorities refused to export monies due Kendall & Sharp on the first three printings of Sharp's *Murder in Bermuda*; it finally was agreed that the German publishers would remit to Kendall & Sharp "in kind—kind being 100 cases of the finest Rhine wines."[21]

[20] *Watertown Daily Times*, 27 November 1937. The available facts concerning Claude Kendall's murder strongly suggest to me that the killer was a male hustler whom Kendall picked up at a bar. On hustling in New York in the 1930s see George Chauncey, *Gay New York: Gender, Urban Culture and the Making of the Gay Male World, 1890-1940* (New York: Basic Books, 1994), 191-192.
[21] *New York Times Book Review*, 24 February 1935.

After eight decades, Willoughby Sharp's excellent tales of detection are finally in print again, courtesy of the industrious Coachwhip Publications. So what makes these mysteries appealing to fans of Golden Age crime fiction? *Murder in Bermuda* naturally benefits from the fact that Willoughby Sharp had been living in Bermuda for two years when he wrote the novel. Over the course of the first third of the twentieth century the beautiful island increasingly attracted moneyed American tourists. "As elite tourism gave way to mass tourism," notes one scholar, "America's wealthy went further afield. In addition to its sandy beaches and temperate year-round climate, Bermuda had the distinct advantage of being an island colony. Ordinary Americans could not hop into their cars and drive there." Ordinary, homebound Americans, however, could read about Bermuda in Willoughby Sharp's novel.[22]

One of the most surprising things about Bermuda that non-Bermudans would have learned from perusing *Murder in Bermuda* is that motor cars were prohibited on the island in the 1930s. At the behest of writer Mark Twain, future United States president Woodrow Wilson had drawn up a petition of prominent American tourists of Bermuda, requesting that automobiles be banned from the island, on the grounds that auto traffic on the island was offensive "to persons of taste and cultivation." Knowing who buttered their bread, so to speak, Bermudans with the 1908 Motor Car Bill banned all motorized vehicles on the island. This prohibition was not repealed until 1946. During the years the Motor Car Bill held sway, Bermudans were limited for transportation either to horse and buggy or bicycle until 1931, when a single line railway running from St. George's to Somerset by way of Hamilton was completed. All these forms of transport, including the recently completed railway, make their appearances in *Murder in Bermuda*.[23]

In addition to the appealing local color Sharp provides in *Murder in Bermuda*, readers also will discover in the book's pages an

[22] Steven High, *Base Colonies in the Western Hemisphere, 1940-1967* (New York: Palgrave Macmillan, 2009), 45-46.
[23] High, *Base Colonies*, 45-46; "The Years of Change 1930-1979," *Bermuda Police History*, at http://www.bermudapoliceservice.bm/node/102.

interesting puzzle and a pleasingly realistic depiction of police procedure. *Bermuda* details the police investigation that occurs after Constable Simmons, on the morning before Easter, discovers a woman's lifeless body on Snake Road. The woman has been stabbed to death. Incongruously, a bouquet of lilies lies by her side. From the slender clue of the Easter lilies an intricately interlaced murder problem quickly blossoms. The Bermuda police are shocked to find that a murder has occurred on their peaceful isle. "Damn it, Simmons!" laments Inspector McNear. "What's this island coming to when a girl's not safe on the highway?" Today the inspector's plaint seems rather quaint, no doubt, but in fact Bermuda was known in the 1930s for its paucity of violent crime (bootlegging was not counted as such, of course). "There has never been a murder in Bermuda in my time—not among our white people at least," reflects a worried Chief of Police Masters. "I ask you to think of the most unpleasant publicity if we admitted it to be murder! Think how the interests of the island would suffer!" Yet murder it inarguably proves, much to the mortification of Masters. Soon another person is found dead, a man this time. He has been polished off in Hamilton, the territorial capital, by means of a favored 1920s poison, mercury bichloride. "If there's another crime in Hamilton I'm going to move to Chicago," announces one islander.[24]

It becomes apparent that the rash of criminal mayhem in Bermuda may be connected to the abduction of a young child in the United States. Surely Willoughby Sharp was influenced to include this plot element in his novel by the notorious Lindbergh kidnapping case of 1932, which also famously inspired Agatha Christie's

[24] Willoughby Sharp, *Murder in Bermuda* (1933; rept., Greenville, OH: Coachwhip, 2013), p. 122. On mercury bichloride deaths in the 1920s see "Popular Poisons Part II: Mercury Bichloride," *Mary Miley's Roaring Twenties: A Unique Decade in American History*, at http://marymiley.wordpress.com/2009/08/15/popular-poisons-part-ii-mercury-bichloride/. "It is said that there has never been a murder in Bermuda," the notice for *Murder in Bermuda* in the *New York Times Book Review* noted sardonically, "but since the island has become a favorite resort of Americans, a people notoriously addicted to homicide, there is no telling what may happen in days to come." *New York Times Book Review*, 27 August 1933.

Murder on the Orient Express (1934). Interestingly, Sharp, a scion of American wealth and privilege with young children of his own, allowed himself a bit of acid social commentary concerning the markedly unequal attention afforded by the American press in a depression-wracked decade to the tragedies of the rich and the poor. "Quite typical of a rich, individualistic nation in which fifteen million men, with their wives and children, were undergoing various stages of starvation," he wrote caustically, "the kidnapping of little Marcia Marsden from the Fifth Avenue home of her fabulously wealthy parents had filled the front sheets of America's daily newspapers until even the stirring foreign political news was crowded to an inside page."[25]

Happily, in Sharp's fictional mystery tale the dark tragedy that enshrouded the Lindbergh family is averted and his puzzle, which involves some clever authorial sleights-of-hand, is solved—not by some preternaturally gifted amateur detective who happens to be visiting Bermuda, it should be added, but by the dogged local police force. *Murder in Bermuda* actually is an early police procedural crime novel, in that the book focuses on the investigatory activities not of one Great Detective, but rather an entire police force. To be sure, three men predominate: Chief of Police Masters, Superintendent Welch and Inspector McNear. It is Welch who has the keenest insights into the crimes, yet several men have their moments to shine, including Constable Simmons, the only black cop we get to see in action in the tale.[26]

The reviewer in the Book of the Week column of *The Harvard Crimson* perceptively noted the unusual emphasis on police detail

[25] Sharp, *Bermuda*, p. 62.

[26] Constable Simmons appears to have been partly inspired by Charles Edward Simons, who had been appointed Bermuda's first Detective Officer in 1919 and "soon became a familiar figure to one and all as he pedal cycled around the island investigating crime." See "The Early Years 1609-1929," *Bermuda Police History*, at http://www.bermudapoliceservice.bm/node/101. By 1933, Bermuda had a police force that numbered seventy-five individuals, "two-thirds of whom were expatriate Englishmen." See "The Years of Change 1930-1979," *Bermuda Police History*, at http://www.bermudapoliceservice.bm/node/102.

in *Murder in Bermuda*: "The pleasant variation from the general mystery story is the manner in which the various police officers working upon the case help each other and together see the thing through, so that in this story, instead of the one stereotyped super sleuth very nobly carrying on, we have the small group solve their problem by their cooperative efforts." The reviewer also highly praised the novel more generally, noting especially its "welcome freshness and originality" and the technical assurance of its author: "[Sharp] utilizes all the long-accepted conventions of the mystery story, but he does so with such ingenuity and creates such a welter of involved circumstances that we are almost entirely unaware of his technical trickery."[27]

A chorus of American reviewers echoed this *Crimson* laudation. "Willoughby Sharp has produced an entertaining yarn with enough legitimately misleading clues scattered through it to keep the reader guessing wrong most of the time," declared the notice in the *New York Times Book Review*. Joining in the hymn of praise, the reviewer for the Albany, New York, *Knickerbocker Press* avowed that the novel was "as complicated and satisfying a mystery as one could hope to find." On the other side of the United States in California, the *Sacramento Bee* reviewer concurred, confidently asserting that any reader would be "loath to lay down [*Murder in Bermuda*] until the final page is completed."[28]

Willoughby Sharp's second detective novel, *Murder of the Honest Broker*, maintains the standard of *Murder in Bermuda*, again offering readers an interesting, authentically depicted setting for violent death, as well as an intriguing fair play puzzle. *Broker* takes us back to the United States, to a very different locale from *Bermuda*, yet, withal, one with which Willoughby Sharp was quite familiar: the New York Stock Exchange. In his review of the novel in the *Daily Oklahoman*, Todd Downing suggested that Sharp had caught the temper of the times: "It's axiomatic with mystery

[27] "In Bermuda," *The Harvard Crimson*, 28 October 1933.

[28] These reviews snippets are drawn from the back panel of the Claude Kendall edition of *Murder of the Honest Broker*.

writers that readers like to vent spleen vicariously upon the corpse, so what's more welcome these days than a nice, well-fed financier?"[29]

In *Murder of the Honest Broker*, the generous Willoughby Sharp actually provided, for the delighted Depression-era reader's delectation, the corpses of not one, but two, well-fed financiers. Continuing the streak of originality he had exhibited in *Murder in Bermuda*, he also introduced a new lead detective: Inspector Bullock, an acerbic, tough guy New York cop who is amusingly endowed with an abiding aversion to the great cloud of fictional gentleman amateur sleuths, such as Philo Vance, Ellery Queen and Drury Lane, that plagues the New York police force, snapping up every last clue like hungry locusts. "I'd like to run up against one of those mincing, namby-pamby, know-it-alls just once," cries Bullock. "Detectives! Bah! They and their Egyptian mummies and stuffed fish and their underground passages and their slant-eyed Chinese hatchet men. They give me a great big pain and I'll give you one guess where!"[30]

The "honest broker" of the title is the prominent New York stockbroker Philip Torrent. He dramatically dies on the floor of the Stock Exchange, from some form of poison. Another broker, Sandy Harrison, expires in his office at the Exchange only a few minutes later. Bizarrely, he too has been poisoned. "Don't tell me it's a strange, oriental poison known only to the high priests of an obscure tribe in the upper Himalayas," Inspector Bullock sarcastically advises the Medical Examiner. "Don't tell me that, 'cause I'm way behind on my Fu-Manchu stories."[31]

[29] Evans, *Clues and Corpses*, p. 258.
[30] Willoughby Sharp, *Murder of the Honest Broker* (1934; rept, Greenville, OH: Coachwhip Publications, 2013), p. 52. Bullock's comments reference S. S. Van Dine's Philo Vance detective novels, *The Scarab Murder Case* (1930) and *The Dragon Murder Case* (1933), as well as the Dr. Fu Manchu mystery thrillers written by Sax Rohmer and possibly Alexandra David-Neel's *Magic and Mystery in Tibet* (1932), perhaps the most successful non-fiction book published by Claude Kendall. This latter book was also referenced in two highly praised 1938 mysteries by Clyde B. Clason and Clayton Rawson, *The Man from Tibet* and *Death from a Top Hat*.
[31] Sharp, *Broker*, p. 59.

Just *how* the two men were poisoned is as a tricky question as *who* was behind it. Certainly there is no shortage of murder suspects in the case of Philip Torrent. At least a half-dozen people had motives for his murder: the brokerage partner, who has been defrauding Torrent; the unfaithful wife, who has been carrying on an affair; the unfaithful wife's broker boyfriend, who is angry that Torrent will not give her a divorce; the debauched nephew, who wants the money that Torrent holds in trust for him; the discarded mistress, who still carries a torch for Torrent; and the speakeasy partner, who finds it extremely inconvenient at the moment to return Torrent's investment funds. But who had a motive to kill Sandy Harrison as well? It adds up to a tricky problem for Inspector Bullock, who at no point in his investigation spares tears for the stockbroker murder victims. This is Bullock's response when he first hears of the deaths of the two men:

> "Two members of the Stock exchange have been poisoned."
>
> "Whee!" whistled the Inspector. "Ain't that what they call the perfect crime? Somebody beat me to it! I've had my eye on that job myself ever since the time I lost five hundred dollars in Anaconda Copper back in '29."[32]

Inspector Bullock emphatically is no respecter of persons, be they of high or low social station. On one occasion he makes his class resentment clear to Mr. Barton, an assistant secretary of the Stock Exchange:

[32] Ibid, p. 53. Inspector Bullock refers to a late 1920s boom and bust cycle in the values of Anaconda Copper shares, which wiped out the savings of many small investors. The losses were blamed on a share pushing scheme by Percy Rockefeller and other tycoons. See Lucy Moore, *Anything Goes: A Biography of the Roaring Twenties* (New York: The Overlook Press, 2010). Obviously Sharp, who was on the New York Stock Exchange at the time, would have been well aware of what was going on behind the financial curtain, so to speak.

> "Will the head waiter be there [at the Luncheon Club] now?" asked Bullock. "It's 5 o'clock."
>
> "Yes," smiled Barton. "It's another one the blessings of Repeal [of Prohibition]. This time two years ago the Club was deserted after three o'clock but now the members like to linger in our new bar and lately they've even taken to ordering their dinners there."
>
> "That's a funny thing," said Inspector Bullock. "The exact same thing happened in my club, the McGillogolly Social Association of Brooklyn. Lately we've had to throw the boys out on their pants at the closing hour."
>
> Mr. Barton's face lost its affable smile. "Oh, yes, quite," he finally managed to reply.[33]

Bullock is similarly *direct* with his subordinates:

> "That you, Mulligan? Your troubles aren't over. Go back to the Alden Apartments, sit downstairs in the lobby and if that girl goes out tonight you stick to her tighter than a chorus girl's brassiere."[34]

Love him or hate him, Willoughby Sharp's Inspector Bullock is, as they used to say, *a real live wire* (and he does in fact solve what turns out to be for him a frustratingly bookish case, though only after consulting the *Encyclopedia Britannica*). Admittedly, the other characters in *Broker* are more in the nature of stock, although it is gratifying to see that Philip Torrent's speakeasy partner, Chipo Marinelli, is one of the rarest of things in Golden Age Anglo-American mystery, an Italian male who does not spend all his time speaking in painfully exaggerated dialect, gesticulating wildly and threatening people with death by stiletto. In both *Bermuda* and *Broker* Sharp commendably refrains from crudely

[33] Sharp, *Broker*, p. 77.
[34] Ibid, pp. 96-97.

caricaturing individuals belonging to racial/ethnic groups that stand outside the WASP charmed circle.

Like *Bermuda*, *Broker* garnered good critical notices. The take in *Kirkus Reviews*—"Good reading and an ingenious solution"—was echoed in the *New York Times Book Review*, which pronounced: "An amusing yarn and a puzzling one." For fans of classical detection, a delighted Todd Downing avowed, reading *Murder of an Honest Broker* was "like meeting a long lost friend."[35]

For 1935 Willoughby Sharp had promised detective fiction devotees that he would deliver another Inspector Bullock adventure, *The Mystery of the Multiplying Mules*, yet it never appeared, despite being advertised by Claude Kendall as a soon-to-be-published book. Certainly the title is intriguing, as is the brief description of the plot given in Claude Kendall promotional material: "Inspector Bullock is called in by the Logans not because something has been stolen, but because something has been added to their household. On three successive Friday mornings they have found in their locked barn, mingling with their own animals, two strange mules. Before the reason for the multiplying mules is found, three deaths follow in rapid order." Sadly, crime fiction fans up to this day have never yet been able to learn how Inspector Bullock mastered the mystifying matter of those multiplying mules. Perhaps one day Sharp's manuscript will suddenly appear (assuming it ever in fact existed).

After retiring from the crime fiction field and his publishing venture with Claude Kendall in 1936, Willoughby Sharp lived for two more decades. In 1943 he joined the Research Institute of America as an account executive. When, after a long illness, he passed away in New York City in 1956, he was a member of the Research institute's executive staff. Sharp's best-known contribution to posterity, however, surely is his son, also named William Willoughby Sharp, who was born in 1936, the same year that his

[35] *Kirkus Reviews*, 10 August 1934; *New York Times Review*, 19 August 1934; Evans, *Clues and Corpses*, p. 258.

father left Kendall & Sharp. The younger Willoughby Sharp, who died in 2008, was an internationally renowned conceptual artist.[36]

The elder Sharp's two murder mysteries were never reprinted in paperback after their initial appearances in the United States in 1933 and 1934, respectively, and, as we have seen, Sharp's publisher, Claude Kendall, met his own violent demise at malign hands in 1937. If ever an author had seemed to have dropped into the pit of artistic annihilation, surely it was Willoughby Sharp. But seasoned mystery fans know to expect surprise endings and here, happily, they now have one. The delightfully devious detective fiction of Willoughby Sharp has returned from the dead, to entertain a new generation of discriminating classical mystery fans.

[36] See "Willoughby Sharp, 72, Versatile Avant-Gardist, Is Dead," *New York Times*, 30 December 2008.

MURDER OF AN HONEST BROKER

1
THE MAN EVERYONE LIKED

"These are the facts, Mr. Torrent," the auditor repeated grimly. "Your partner has stolen from you the sum of three hundred and eighty thousand two hundred and forty-seven dollars—"

"Impossible," snapped Torrent. "Why I—"

"—and sixty-two cents," completed the auditor with stern finality.

He re-arranged his papers in a neat pile on the desk. "Figures sometimes—yes, usually—lie; but this statement—unlike those which your partner has been supplying you,—tells the truth. There's not a shadow of doubt as to its correctness."

The man behind the broad oak desk gave a signal of dismissal. The auditor silently left the room. For a full minute Philip Torrent sat motionless, staring fixedly at the heavily paneled walls of his elaborately equipped office; his eyes were unseeing, his head rested on up-propped arms.

The stock-ticker at his side came suddenly to life with a series of staccato clicks. The tape unrolled, TESTING . . . . TESTING . ABCDEFGHI . AAA . . . . . BBB . . . . . 1234567890 . . . . . Even this insistent reminder of the inescapable present failed to rouse him from his reverie.

The whole situation was untrue, unthinkable, unbelievable. Temple Hastings, his partner of fifteen years, could not be a thief. And yet there could be no mistake. Fifteen years is an aeon in Wall Street, where changes in fortune and prestige occur with lightning rapidity. Yet these years had seen the stock-exchange firm of

Torrent & Hastings wax rich and powerful while the ups and downs of the market only seemed to strengthen the partnership's already impregnable position.

And now these unexpected and terrible revelations meant the end. Not the end in the old melodramatic usage of the word for the loss of his money would be of far less moment to Torrent than the loss of his implicit trust in his old friend. It did mean, however, the end of the honorable life of *Torrent & Hastings* as well as it spelt a complete retrenchment in his personal life. After winding up the affairs of the firm he would have little left save his seat on the Exchange; but that dull ache in his heart came from sorrow over the present rather than fear of the future.

Torrent bent further over his desk. The ticker broke the silence once more. NEW . YORK . STOCK . EXCHANGE . MARCH . 31 . 1935 . The machine paused and seemed to wait with the eager impatience of a thoroughbred anxious to be off.

Torrent suddenly lifted his head. His crisp gray hair hung untidily over his rugged forehead; his blue eyes had lost their unseeing stare. He pressed a call-button and presently a clerk appeared.

"Has Mr. Hastings arrived yet?" he inquired.

"No, sir, Mr. Hastings telephoned he'd gone to White Plains for the day."

Torrent grunted sourly and waved the boy away. That was typical of his partner's easy-going attitude toward life. To be able to go off to a game of golf, and to put out of mind any thoughts of the inevitable day of reckoning was to Hastings an easy procedure.

An electric clock on the wall began to strike. With a muttered exclamation Torrent rose hastily from his chair, put on his hat, walked into the board room where customers sat expectantly awaiting the opening of the market, exchanged a parting word with his manager, left his offices and made his way down the corridor to the elevator. A minute later he crossed the ground floor lobby, nodded to the bulky gray-clad guards and entered the Stock Exchange.

II

AT ALMOST the same moment Mrs. Philip Torrent awoke from a troubled sleep, yawned, stretched languidly and finally rang for her maid.

"Margaret," she inquired when the servant's trim figure appeared in the doorway, "have there been telephone messages?"

"Yes, madam. Mr. McDonald called. He desires that you telephone him at once."

Mary Torrent motioned toward a near-by closet and the maid glided over to return with a fluffy bed-jacket. She arranged the lacy garment around the bare shoulders of her mistress and disappeared kitchenwards.

Mrs. Torrent spent a satisfying moment powdering her nose, which was exceedingly beautiful; rouging her lips, which were exceedingly provocative, and arranging her hair, which was exceedingly blond; then, prepared for her conversation, she dialed a number and lay back on her silken pillows with a little sigh of contentment. When a voice answered she lifted herself from the bed and pressed her lips in a caressing gesture close to the telephone.

"Jack, darling, I'm sorry I slept so late but I was so exhausted—so worried, I—"

"What did he say?" demanded the other.

"He won't do it," Mary Torrent answered. "He refuses a divorce on any grounds."

There was a sinister silence. "He'll have to, by God," the man cried out at last. "He'll have to give you up or I'll—"

"Hush, darling," soothed the woman. "We'll find a way."

"You've been saying that for more than a year. I don't mind telling you, Mary, I'm fed up with the situation—something will have to be done—and soon!"

Mary Torrent broke into tears. "Oh, Jack, Jack, I know how you feel, but you must—"

"Do you love me, Mary?"

"You know I do!"

"Will you go away with me today?"

"No, dear."

"Why?"

"I've told you a thousand times. It must be divorce or nothing."

The voice at the other end seemed far away as she heard her last words repeated.

"Divorce or nothing—"

A long pause followed. "But there is an alternative," McDonald concluded slowly.

The woman caught her breath with a sharp gasp.

"Jack, you don't—you wouldn't—"

The click of the disconnection was her only answer.

III

"FILL 'ER UP again, Chipo," ordered the young man. "I'm going to get good and drunk today." Chipo smiled somberly and placed a bottle of Scotch whisky before his customer.

"Go ahead, have your fun. It's one of the last drinks you'll have here. Drink up, but tomorrow's the day Chipo Marinelli gets drunk."

Mournfully the Italian gazed down the bar lined with its regiment of bottles. "Tomorrow the new license laws come in and then my profits end."

"Ah, come on, Chipo; it isn't as bad as all that. You can get a license and go on the same as ever. What're you worrying about?"

Chipo shook his head vigorously. "I ain't in the same boat as some of the swell speaks. I ain't kidding myself. Some one down at the State Liquor Authority has it in for me and won't give me a license. And besides, people are going back more and more to the hotels and we'll have to go out of business. The rich mob don't come here any more, I know them—they're—they're fickle—that's the word. It was dear old Chipo once, but it's Chipo who-the-hell-cares after tomorrow. Ever since the law was changed to let people stand at hotel bars, there hasn't been any reason for them to go to speaks anymore."

"People are used to speaks," remonstrated his customer. "They'll still come."

"No, they came here in the old days to get drunk—not to look at any decorations—and they stayed to meals on account they were cheap and good. But my chefs, they all leave. They get back the fine jobs—Waldorf, Sherry, Plaza—all the swell hotels take them back. Our good food—zoop—it is gone!"

The young man laughed. "Well, for your sake, Chipo, I hope things won't be as blue as all that."

The Italian shrugged his shoulders expressively and made no reply.

The customer continued to drink his whisky while the proprietor gloomily busied himself in arranging the back-bar in anticipation of the luncheon trade. Deftly he prepared a long row of old-fashioned cocktail set-ups. The sugar, the bitters, the cherries and the slices of orange joined each other in the hospitable squat glasses.

The door leading from the bar to the dining-room opened and a man entered.

"Morning, Chipo," the newcomer greeted cheerfully.

The proprietor grunted. "A fine time to come to work, Joe. It's after ten o'clock. All your work you leave for me."

Joe grinned good-naturedly, stepped behind the bar, donned his white coat and adjusted his apron As Marinelli left the room, still grumbling to himself, the tardy bartender gave the lone customer a surreptitious wink.

"In a bad humor, eh?"

"You can hardly blame him," was the reply. "He has lots to worry about."

The bartender waved his arms in a wide gesture of derision.

"Don't worry. Chipo will land on his feet. He's a smart one. He's always crying poor, but I'll bet he has plenty of what-it-takes tucked away somewhere."

If the barman could have peeked at that moment into a room directly above, he would have heard a conversation that would more than have borne out his statement.

"Here's the message," said Chipo to his wife, Maria. "Mr. Torrent wants his money—tomorrow!"

The girl read the contents slowly. Her black eyes smoldered and her hand shook as she returned the letter to her husband. She was a handsome woman of a more Spanish than Italian type; short, sturdily built and with closely cropped dark hair.

"What'll we do, Chipo?" she asked.

The man did not reply.

"How much is it in all?" demanded Maria.

"The house—it cost sixty thousand—half is his, and from profits there comes to him forty thousand more."

"Oh, Chipo, Chipo!" wailed the woman. "What can we do? You've lost so much at the races and playing the stock market, we'll have nothing left after we've paid him."

A cold, brooding look gleamed for a moment in her husband's eyes. His large fingers were opening and shutting spasmodically. He looked through rather than at her when he answered.

"Nobody knows Philip Torrent owns half of this place but us," he whispered slowly, "—nobody, he told me so himself."

The man's voice had a hard, metallic sound; his lips were set at an unpleasant angle as he completed his sentence.

"—Suppose something suddenly happened to Mr. Torrent?"

IV

"NOW PLEASE try to be reasonable, Lucy," begged Philip Torrent. "The thing was inevitable. It might as well come now."

Lucy Laverne's blue eyes snapped dangerously. "That's fine talk, Philip. It's easy enough for you to slip out like this. But how about me? I'm to be thrown out like a stray cat."

Torrent toyed for a moment with the *omelet Bourguignonne* that lay untouched on the silver platter before him. He carefully conveyed half of the golden concoction to his plate before he answered her question.

"You're being melodramatic, my dear," he observed at last. "Such a situation could never occur. You and I have been dear friends for five years. During that time, if I say so myself, you have been more than amply provided for. Your bank manager, I am sure, would tell you there is no big, bad wolf lurking around *your* door."

The woman leaned across the table. Her voice when she spoke again was vibrant with suppressed passion.

"It isn't only the money, Philip—although we'll speak of that later—it's you, don't you understand—Can't you understand? You have been my whole life. I can't and shan't give you up."

Her hand shot fiercely across the table to grasp Torrent's wrist. "Who is she? Is it that dirty little chit at the Frivolity?"

Torrent smiled wanly. "There isn't any little chit—dirty or clean."

"Then why?" she demanded.

"For two reasons, Lucy. First, I've lost a great deal of money and I can't afford to go on as before. Secondly, my wife is trying to get a divorce. This I am determined she shall never have. To prevent it my own conduct must be beyond reproach."

Lucy Laverne smiled sarcastically. "You're starting late," she informed her companion.

"I shall follow a certain old adage," he replied, "I'm a firm believer in clichés."

The woman drew her chair nearer the table. There was a sudden glitter in her eyes—a gleam that only a psycho-pathologist would have recognized.

"Well, here's another cliché to add to your collection. If you do this to me you will live just long enough to regret it."

Torrent appeared completely unmoved. He glanced at his watch and motioned to the waiter.

"It's after two o'clock," he said to the girl. "I must return to the Exchange. I'm sorry you've taken this inevitable break-up so much to heart, but as far as I'm concerned our affair is finished."

V

AT THREE O'CLOCK a chauffeur drove a shining black Packard slowly down Broad Street and drew up before the ornate façade of the Stock Exchange. Torrent, who had been standing at an entrance, bade goodbye to a group of fellow brokers and entered his car.

"To the Metropolis Club," he directed his chauffeur.

He leaned back in the soft cushions and lit a cigarette. What a day! The terrible revelation concerning his partner, Temple Hastings; the uncomfortable lunch with Lucy Laverne; and then the distressingly weak market in the afternoon. As the automobile picked its way slowly up Broadway he looked forward with unusual anticipation to a quiet game of bridge at his club. For tomorrow with its inevitable showdown with Hastings would hold in store more disagreeable experiences than even this wretched day.

Presently the car drew up at the hospitable portals of the Metropolis Club, and, with a nod to the ancient doorman, he entered, divested himself of his overcoat and hat, and hurried upstairs to the card room.

He played with indifferent success for several hours. Indeed the question of gain or loss was of small consequence to him. For today, relaxation and freedom from thoughts of the future were the only requisites.

Presently, a rubber having been completed, his seat was claimed by a late-comer and Torrent wandered into the crowded bar. He joined a little group of cronies and soon was beaming over his third cocktail.

As he stood there a club servant approached and whispered in his ear. "Your nephew is calling, sir."

Torrent made an impatient gesture and moodily followed the attendant down the corridor. More trouble, that was certain. Interviews with his dead brother's dissipated son invariably resulted in harsh words and harder feelings.

In the Strangers' room, Torrent found his nephew sprawled untidily on a wide leather lounge.

One look told him that the boy, as usual, was hopelessly intoxicated.

"Well, Howard?"

The young man remained seated. His watery eyes tried vainly to focus on the bulky figure of his uncle.

"You know what I want—money!" he stated thickly.

His uncle regarded him with increasing disfavor.

"You had your monthly allowance two weeks ago. If you've spent it already that's your own look-out. You can't expect me to be continually giving you extra funds so that you can persist in your obvious ambition which is to drink dry every hotel, restaurant and speak-easy in the city."

"It's my own money," stormed Howard Torrent. "Damn you—it's my own money to do with as I like!"

"Young man," replied his uncle, "your father knew you well enough to make me the trustee of your estate. If you had been left in control of your money it would have long since been squandered. You are receiving a very adequate allowance. While I live it will not be increased until you have shaken yourself together and become a man instead of a sot!"

Philip Torrent strode angrily across the room and touched a bell-button. An attendant entered.

"My nephew is leaving," he curtly informed the man.

"Very good, sir.'

A moment later the front door closed discreetly behind the disheveled Howard Torrent.

Back in the bar Philip Torrent picked up his unfinished cocktail and drained the contents with a gulp. He signaled to the barman.

"Bring another Martini to the card room."

He turned, nodded to a group of new arrivals who greeted him jovially with much back-slapping, and regaled him for a few minutes with the latest risqué stock-exchange joke. Finally he broke away in the direction of the card room.

"Philip isn't looking his best," observed one of the group he had just quitted.

"If he isn't—he ought to be," replied one of the others. "I would say that Philip Torrent is the luckiest of fellows—rich, good-looking and popular. I'd bet my bottom dollar that *he's* one person who hasn't an enemy in the world."

2
MURDER ON THE STOCK EXCHANGE

THE TWO MEN stood facing each other belligerently.

"Well, what do you propose to do about it?" demanded Temple Hastings.

"Just as much as I can—which unfortunately isn't very much. The partnership laws of the state—You know them as well as I—probably better," Torrent added grimly. "As it is I can't send you to jail, but I have already advised the Exchange of the early dissolution of this partnership. Afterwards I shall inform the governing committee of your actions. I think they will know how to deal with you."

Torrent picked up his hat and turned toward the door. "If you're wise you'll stay here in the office. The Stock Exchange floor won't be large enough for the two of us today."

It was still twenty minutes before the opening of the Exchange but to Torrent the atmosphere of his offices was intolerable. Every desk, every picture on the walls, even the familiar faces of the busy clerks, brought to mind his many years' close association with his faithless partner and conjured up a thousand reminiscences which he vainly tried to forget. On the Exchange, at least, he could rid himself of these surging memories.

Soon he was walking across the huge, high-ceilinged trading-floor to a booth against the west wall where a row of telephones connected his far-flung offices to the Exchange. His two clerks, pencils in hand, were busily writing down the overnight accumulation of buying and selling orders that had flooded in from near and far.

Torrent picked up a thick sheaf of orders which one of his clerks had just received over the telephone.

"I'll give these to the specialists myself," he told the boy, who gaped at his employer with undisguised astonishment.

"They're all far away from the market, sir. It'd be a waste of time for you, sir. Hadn't I better have a page boy distribute them?"

Torrent smiled genially. "I feel like doing a little unnecessary work—I'll attend to them."

The clerk gazed after the broker's retreating form.

"Well, I'll be damned," he exclaimed to his companion. "I've worked for the old man for twelve years now and that's the first time I ever saw him even look at anything less than a thousand-share market order."

Torrent slowly strolled from trading post to trading post, giving the order-slips to the specialists who were busily entering notations in their order books. At the General Motors post his cousin, Berkley Warner, took him by the arm and led him a little aside.

"Philip—I don't want to be a tattle-tale, but I thought you might be interested. Last night I saw Lucy Laverne at El Morocco with young Sandy Harrison."

There was a moment's silence.

"It's all right by me," Torrent finally said.

"You mean you don't care if she runs around?" the other demanded incredulously. "I thought you were rather fussy on the subject?"

"That's true—I was—once. But it really doesn't matter. The whole thing is cold turkey now— You understand?"

Warner nodded slowly. "Yes, I understand and I'm sorry. She's a nice kid—Lucy."

"Don't be so melodramatic," laughed Torrent. "It was all very amicably arranged. Tell me," he went on, changing the subject abruptly, "did Lucy and Sandy seem to be enjoying themselves?"

His companion broke into loud laughter. "Well, hardly! The last I saw of them she had just finished scratching one whole side of his face with her finger nails."

"Poor fellow," sympathized Torrent. "I feel sorry for him. Lucy's very proud of her nice, sharp, red nails. Sandy won't be around for a week or more."

"Oh, yes, he will," replied Warner. "There he is over there."

The two men turned simultaneously and followed Sandy Harrison's progress across the Exchange. As he passed a group of young brokers he was greeted with a chorus of resounding boos.

"Oh, Sandy—Sandy—what did she do to you?" someone called.

Harrison blushed a deep crimson and continued on his way with as much dignity as he was able to call to his aid.

Even Torrent could not refrain from joining in the laughter. "There's no alibi for nail scratches," he told his cousin. "Their appearance is singularly unique. Even the dull razor blade excuse doesn't fit the bill."

Meanwhile the Exchange grew more and more crowded as a steady stream of brokers, pages and clerks came surging through the many entrances.

High up on the north and south walls the huge annunciators, two gargantuan blackboards, clicked and clacked as varied numbers appeared, called brokers to their telephones, and disappeared once the urgent summons had been answered.

As the hour of ten approached, the crescendo of voices gradually assumed a shriller tone. With each successive minute the scale seemed to rise an octave higher. The gray-clad pages scurried hither and thither, last-second orders clutched in perspiring hands. There was something electric in the air—as if a huge creature was slowly coming to life. Around the trading posts little groups of brokers gathered; stock-sale reporters stood waiting to feed quotations to the maw of the restless ticker; specialists hurriedly entered in their books a never-ending list of newly-arrived commissions; telephones tinkled, buzzed and shrilled in every conceivable key; feet quickened; a great bell boomed; the tumult rose ten octaves higher—the Stock Exchange was open.

II

Jack McDonald continued speaking while Torrent eyed him with unconcealed distaste.

"—therefore, since your wife has told you she loves me, I should think you would be man enough to step gracefully out of her life."

Torrent laughed and shrugged his shoulders carelessly,

"If every husband stepped, as you call it, gracefully out of the picture each time his wife conceived a passing fancy for young men like yourself, the divorce courts would have to be open night as well as day."

"My love for Mary is more than a passing fancy," retorted McDonald hotly.

"Time alone will tell," Torrent told him, "and time is precisely the medicine with which I propose to cure my wife of this infatuation."

"That is your final word?" demanded the younger man.

"It most certainly is!"

McDonald flared up angrily. "You'll regret your decision."

"It's possible," admitted Torrent, "but on the whole highly improbable."

He pushed back his chair and rose to his feet. "I see no useful purpose in the continuance of a conversation which can only be painful to us both. If you will excuse me—"

Torrent walked abruptly from the corner of the lounge of the Luncheon Club where they had been sitting and headed in the direction of the elevators. As he passed near the bar he hesitated for a moment, then entered. There he sat for some minutes over coffee and a liqueur.

For a man who had just had an extremely distasteful interview with his wife's lover he felt singularly unruffled. He tried to analyze his precise feelings in the matter. After all, he asked himself, did he really love his wife? Had this wave of jealousy that had suddenly overcome him, brought back an affection and love which he had long considered dead? Or was the sensation merely one of rage at McDonald's effrontery in calmly demanding that he should procure an immediate divorce?

At last, after much soul-searching, he admitted to himself that the only one of his susceptibilities which had really been touched was that variable emotion called pride.

III

THE HANDS of the great clock in the Stock Exchange annex stood rigidly at two o'clock as Torrent left the Luncheon Club and took the elevator down to the trading floor. There he found an increased bustle and flurry which, to his experienced eyes, meant that a more active market had developed during his luncheon hour. He glanced up at one of the magnified ticker-tapes that, halfway up the opposite wall, showed, in foot-high letters, the course of the market. What he saw there caused him to quicken his steps in the direction of his clerks. International Air-Conditioning, which was by way of being one of his firm's particular pets, was, in the parlance of financial writers, boiling over. On the tickers, great blocks of IAC were appearing in an almost constant stream and at rapidly rising prices.

His head clerk greeted him excitedly. "Air-Conditioning, sir, it's up ten points."

"Have we been doing anything in it?" inquired Torrent calmly.

"We sure have. We started the buying. We've bought 12,000 shares so far."

"Ring the office," Torrent directed the boy. "Get me the manager."

A moment later the connection was made. "Who's buying all the Air-Conditioning?" There was a pause. "Sounds like he ought to know what he's doing," Torrent said as the manager finished speaking. "Wire our branch offices. Tell them I think it's a good thing."

At Post No. 7 where the shares of International Air-Conditioning, Inc., were dealt in, a thickly-wedged swarm of brokers eddied back and forth. Waving arms and hoarse shouts proclaimed an active market.

From time to time gray-clad pages hurried up, and, edging their way into the whirling mass, emerged a moment later to scurry off across the floor toward the encircling rows of telephones.

Torrent stood on the outskirts of the crowd watching the crest of a wave of buying from the entire country converge on this one spot. As orders reached him from his own office, he elbowed his way in among the other brokers, speedily executed his commissions and returned to his place on the fringe of the crowd. As the closing hour approached a last batch of orders was pressed into his hands. With but a few seconds remaining he dashed back into the crowd.

"I'll give 40 for 5000," he shouted.

An excited roar came from around about. Forty was International Air-Conditioning's high for all time.

A score of brokers jostled and elbowed each other in a frenzied attempt to get closer to Torrent's tall figure.

"Sold you a thousand. Sold you six hundred. Sold fifteen hundred. Sold nine hundred." A chorus of shouts rained down upon him. He scribbled the seller's names on his order pad and rapidly counted up the number of shares he had bought.

"I'll give 40½ for 1000 more—all I need!"

"Sold," snapped a broker.

Torrent glanced over his shoulder and added another name to his list.

The great bell of the Stock Exchange started its closing clamor while the men surrounding Torrent were busily engaged in verifying the trades of the last hectic minute.

"I think we're all straightened out now," said Torrent at last. He put his pencil back in his pocket and gave his clerk a handful of reports.

"A nice day's business, sir," observed the boy.

"Pretty fair," he answered absently. Automatically he took the hat and coat which the clerk offered him and turned toward a nearby doorway.

Suddenly his head jerked back. A horrible distortion appeared on his face. He clutched at his collar as though to tear it off and his breath came in great heaving gasps.

Before the astonished clerk could catch his employer's arm, Torrent's knees seemed to double up and he sank to the floor, lying there in a slowly stiffening heap. One hand worked spasmodically at the neckband of his collar while his left arm turned in a gruesome corkscrew motion until the fingers of the hand had attained an impossible position, twisted and curved against the small of his back.

IV

In the Stock Exchange's private hospital Dr. Martin and his assistant stood looking down on the horribly contorted body.

"Strange—very strange," pointed out Dr. Martin. "It has the appearance of a stroke but the man has plainly choked to death. His respiratory muscles have been entirely paralyzed and death followed from asphyxia."

"But did you ever see a case in which there was a similar position of the head?" urged the assistant. "Look how the head is squared around. Although the body is lying on its back, and the muscles throughout are tense, the face itself is rigidly turned toward the right, while the left arm remains in this curious twisted position."

"Yes—it's a sad problem," stated Dr. Martin morosely, "and a mysterious one."

He turned away from the body and looked out the window down onto the streams of restless humanity eddying in black masses down Wall Street.

"Of course," he finally said, "there'll have to be a post-mortem—whether his family care for it or not. There doesn't seem to be any possibility of foul play, but under the circumstances we *must* find out exactly how Torrent died. I confess I couldn't put my finger at this moment on the exact cause." Dr. Martin strode up and down the room, his hands clasped behind him. He took off his spectacles, carefully cleaned them and replaced them on his angular nose.

"If it weren't absolutely silly," he observed, "I would say that Torrent died of a cobra bite."

"Cobra!" ejaculated the assistant. "Oh, come, that's a bit far-fetched!"

"He had the same symptoms," doggedly persisted his superior. "Exactly!—I remember, when I was quite a young man, I saw a woman in India die from a cobra's bite, and I'm not ever liable to forget it."

The other doctor stroked his small black mustache and judiciously examined his fingertips.

"I hate to disagree, sir," he finally said, "but it looks to me like a simple cardiac condition. The Stock Exchange, after all, isn't the healthiest place in the world for a man of Torrent's years."

"Well," replied Dr. Martin, "we shall soon find out. Do you know I—"

A shrill tinkle of the telephone interrupted his train of thought.

He picked up the receiver. "Dr. Martin speaking—the stretcher bearers, you say—where— Oh, the eleventh floor—right away."

He rang a bell and gave some rapid instructions to the two orderlies who had quickly answered his summons.

"Go up at once to the offices of *Harrison & McGuire.* Young Sandy Harrison has had a fainting spell or a fit—I don't seem to be able to gather anything of intelligence from his secretary who just called me."

The two men hurried off and returned almost immediately bearing a stretcher on which, under a badly concealing blanket, a man writhed in agony.

Dr. Martin slipped off the covering and looked down on the face of Sandy Harrison. He recoiled in horror as he saw the distorted, twitching features, the protruding eyes and livid features.

"My God," he cried out in a choking voice to his assistant. "Look! The same symptoms!"

The unfortunate man was in the midst of a violent tetanic convulsion. Every muscle in his body had sharply contracted; his back was arched so that only his head and feet appeared to be touching the stretcher; the hands were strongly flexed; the jaw clamped shut; the right arm crept slowly under the upraised body with the same slow corkscrew movement the two doctors had observed but a few moments before as Torrent lay dying.

Dr. Martin worked swiftly over his fast weakening patient. Stimulants were given the faltering heart; the stomach pump was freely used. All to no avail. Ten minutes passed and Dr. Martin spread out his hands in a gesture of resignation. One of the orderlies stepped forward and drew a sheet over the mercifully stilled form.

3
ENTER INSPECTOR BULLOCK

Inspector Francis X. Bullock of the Homicide Squad was a great red-faced giant of a man, brusque of speech and direct of manner, and he carried about him none of that sleek aura of hidden knowledge which is the stock in trade of fiction super-detectives.

His comrades at Centre Street had frequently heard him discourse with Irish fluency, causticity and blasphemy on the subject of these mythical and infallible beings.

“I’d like to run up against one of those mincing, namby-pamby, know-it-alls just once. I’d like to put my hands around one of their damned supercilious necks. Detectives! Bah! They and their Egyptian mummies and their stuffed fish and their underground passages and their slant-eyed, Chinese hatchet men. They give me a great big pain and I’ll give you one guess where?”

Luckily Philo Vance, Drury Lane, Thatcher Colt and their comrades were safely protected from Bullock’s wrath behind the staunch, stiff-backed covers of their publishers’ best octavo.

At the Sheriff Street station house Bullock was passing the time of day with his friend, the sergeant-in-charge. The telephone rang urgently and the sergeant picked up the receiver.

“Precinct 11,” he said.

The voice on the other end spoke fast and furiously.

“He is that, sir,” responded the sergeant, all at attention, “and I’ll tell him.”

The sergeant looked down from his elevated desk and jerked a fat finger over his shoulder.

"The old man wants you, Inspector, pronto!" Bullock got up from the chair he had been sitting in so comfortably and wearily stretched his arms. Ten minutes later he was ushered into the office of John Mackay, the Commissioner of Police.

"Afternoon, Bullock," said the chief. "Fine day—fine day!"

"That's right," responded Bullock.

The Police Commissioner leaned across his desk and tapped three times with a pencil on the base of his telephone.

"Inspector, I've got a tough assignment for you."

"They don't make 'em tough enough for me," replied Bullock modestly.

The other smiled sourly.

"Well, we'll see about that. But you may change your tune before long. Now listen to this. There's been two men murdered down at the Stock Exchange."

Bullock's impassive face showed faint signs of interest.

"Holdup?" he inquired.

"No. Nothing like that. Just plain murder. Two members of the Exchange have been poisoned."

"Whee!" whistled the Inspector. "Ain't that what they call the perfect crime? Somebody beat me to it. I've had my eye on that job myself ever since the time I lost five hundred dollars in Anaconda copper back in '29."

The Commissioner of Police remained unsmiling.

"We've got to get busy right away, Inspector, and I don't mean maybe. God only knows what sort of hell may break loose. Those fellows down there have got the pull in this City spelled with a capital P, and they'll want action and plenty of it."

"All right, Chief," said Bullock, mildly. "They'll get it. What's the layout?"

"All we know is that they were poisoned. No one knows how it was done or what with. The bodies are at the Stock Exchange's private hospital. The Chief Medical Examiner will make a preliminary post-mortem there. Get along with you now!"

Inspector Bullock was already moving toward the door. On Lafayette Street he hailed a taxi and headed south bucking the heavy uptown traffic.

Down past City Hall, through the canyon of lower Broadway, the taxi rattled and jerked, finally to pull up at the Wall Street entrance of the Stock Exchange.

Bullock alighted with an agility belying his bulk and hurried into an elevator that speedily deposited him on the hospital floor.

When he entered the main reception room he found a uniformed policeman, notebook in hand, engrossed in tabulating a mass of details. On seeing the Inspector the man saluted and introduced Dr. Martin, the head physician of the Exchange's medical department.

"This is a fine how-do-you-do, Inspector," declared the doctor.

Bullock nodded morosely and demanded, "What was the poison?"

"The Chief Medical Examiner is conducting an autopsy now," replied Dr. Martin. "We should know shortly. The only thing I can tell you for sure is that it wasn't ptomaine poisoning."

"I understand both men died here in the hospital?"

"They did," said Dr. Martin, "and within ten minutes of each other."

"Together when they were stricken?"

"Not at all. They were nowhere near each other when the effects of the poison became apparent. Mr. Torrent was on the Stock Exchange floor while Mr. Harrison was in his office on the tenth floor of this building."

Inspector Bullock surveyed the tip of one of his huge polished boots. "While we're waiting for the Medical Examiner to finish his job," he finally announced, "I'll take a look around the place where Mr. Torrent was poisoned."

He lumbered off toward the door.

Dr. Martin got up hastily from his chair.

"Just a minute, Inspector. Let me get someone to show you around. If you'll wait a moment, I'll have one of the Exchange's assistant secretaries meet you downstairs."

He busied himself with the telephone and presently Bullock departed to be met as arranged by a Mr. Barton, a thin-faced, dignified, sallow-looking man of thirty odd. Together the two walked onto the deserted Stock-Exchange floor.

A dozen porters, equipped with brooms and sundry cleaning materials, were standing listlessly together in the middle of the great room.

Barton pointed a lean finger in their direction. "These fellows usually start cleaning up about three-thirty when all the brokers and clerks have gone. But today we thought it best to hold up their work until the police had a chance to look around."

Bullock grunted. "Darn swell of you; it would have been just too bad if you hadn't!"

He followed his guide across the room, looking about curiously.

"Bit of a mess on this floor of yours," the Inspector observed. "Those porters must have plenty of work to do?"

His companion nodded. "You see, what with brokers, clerks and pages, there's well over two thousand people on the floor here at one time. All these scraps of paper littering up the floor comprise the accumulated trash of five hours—discarded newspapers, order slips and memoranda. During the trading period we have no porters at work and consequently when three o'clock arrives there is plenty of cleaning to do."

"What happens to all the waste paper?" inquired Bullock. "Do you burn it?"

"Oh! No! Nothing as wasteful as all that," denied Mr. Barton. "It's carefully baled in the subbasement and sold to paper dealers. There's about four large bales collected each day."

"Saving bozos, ain't you?" suggested Bullock. "I can remember the days when I'll bet my under-drawers you used to burn all that paper in the furnace."

The young assistant secretary looked uncomfortable. "Times change," he finally agreed.

"Yeah, so I've heard," said the Inspector. "But now where's the place this fellow Torrent was bumped off?"

"Right over here," answered Barton.

The two men stopped alongside the trading post where but an hour before Torrent had watched and aided the meteoric rise of International Air-Conditioning.

"This is where he fell," pointed out Barton.

Bullock circled around the indicated spot and glared down on the unresponsive floor.

"Seems to be more mess here—more scraps of paper and all," he observed to his companion.

"Naturally," he was told, "one of the stocks that's dealt in at this post was the most active on the exchange today."

"Well—and so what?" demanded the Inspector.

The assistant secretary had a patronizing look on his thin face. He explained patiently, "Most active, most people trading. More people trading, more pieces of waste paper lying about. See?"

Bullock wagged his head. "Penetrated," he stated, "penetrated."

His eyes still moodily surveyed the floor. "I'm just enough of a damn ex-flat-foot detective to think there might be some clues in all this obvious mess. Of course, if I was Sherlock Holmes, I'd be able to smell a strange oriental scent wafting about this neighborhood which would put me immediately on the track of a one-armed man from Borneo wearing a gardenia in the buttonhole of a brown tweed suit. But unfortunately— "

The Inspector reached out a long arm toward one of the silent, inactive porters.

"Hey! you! Come over here!"

The man looked inquiringly at Barton who nodded an answer to the unspoken question.

"Now this is what I want," directed Inspector Bullock when the porters had gathered around him. "I want all this paper that's scattered around here picked up and kept separate from the rest of the junk you find around the other parts of the floor. Understand?"

The head porter nodded solemnly.

"I'll be back soon," said Bullock. He pulled his coat aside significantly and displayed his golden shield, "and I'll be seeing you."

"Now where?" he asked the tongue-tied Barton.

"You mean where Harrison—?"

"Yeah."

"Upstairs on the eleventh floor."

Bullock grunted. "Flighty bird this murderer of ours—"

The assistant secretary drew himself up to his full five feet five inches. He did not approve of Bullock's flippancy in the presence of death.

In acid silence Barton led the way once more to the elevators and escorted the Inspector upwards. At the eleventh floor the two men walked down the corridor to stop presently before a pair of large bronze doors marked in golden splendor, HARRISON & McGUIRE.

They walked in. The first person they saw was a girl clerk powdering her nose. She had been crying.

"Police," announced Bullock without a trace of tact.

The girl broke into a new paroxysm of tears.

"Who's in charge here?" the detective demanded.

The girl dabbed ineffectually at her reddened eyes. "Mr. West, the manager, I guess," she finally answered. "I'll get him for you."

Mr. West was a polished little man who shone immaculately from the top of his slicked brown hair to the tips of his glossy boots.

Bullock introduced himself.

"Terrible thing, Inspector, terrible."

"Yeah," said Bullock. "Where did it happen?"

"Mr. Harrison was taken ill in his private office."

"Taken ill, eh?" Bullock looked the manager in the eye. "Just to keep the record straight—Mr. Harrison was murdered!"

"God," said Mr. West. He collapsed into a convenient chair and perspiration glistened on his forehead. "No one could want to kill him!"

"Yeah? Well the proof of the pudding is in the killing," replied Bullock callously. "Where's this room where it happened?"

Shakily the manager got up and led the way through the elaborately equipped offices. He threw open a door and ushered Barton and the Inspector into Harrison's room.

Bullock glanced around. "I'll look through his papers later. Just tell me all you know."

West cleared his throat. "Mr. Harrison arrived here about four minutes after the Exchange closed. There was a young lady waiting to see him and they came together into this room."

"She came on business?" queried Bullock. "I mean for the purpose of giving him orders in stocks or bonds."

"I don't think so. I never saw her before. More likely a lady friend, if you know what I mean."

"Her name?" demanded the Inspector succinctly as he took out his notebook.

"Lucy Laverne."

"And then what happened?"

"They'd been in this room only a few minutes when Miss Laverne came tearing out into the customers' room screaming that Mr. Harrison had had a stroke."

"Then I rushed in and found him stretched out stiff as a board on the floor—just about here." West pointed to a spot near the desk. "Afterwards we telephoned the hospital downstairs and they took him away."

"What happened to Laverne?"

"She carried on something wild, tried to go to the hospital, but they wouldn't let her. Finally she went away."

"Of course no one thought of asking her address, I suppose?" complained the Inspector.

"I don't believe so. The place was in a frightful uproar. We didn't know then there was anything funny about Mr. Harrison's attack, and there was no reason for us to care whether she went or stayed."

"Nobody saw her leave?"

"I don't think so. She just slipped away after they refused to let her go to the hospital."

Bullock turned toward the door. Outside he waited for the two men to join him, then twisted the key in the lock behind him.

"We'll go back to the hospital now. See you later," he told West.

II

THE MEDICAL EXAMINER and Dr. Martin took off their operating gowns and settled down on two comfortable chairs in the reception room.

"You agree?" asked the Medical Examiner.

"Yes," replied Dr. Martin. "But, of course, I've never seen a similar case."

"Nor I," replied the other. "But the tests seem conclusive enough."

"They're absolutely conclusive. There can be no possible doubt, in spite of the unusualness of the poison."

The two men sat silent for a moment.

"I seem to remember an attempt on the life of an English statesman by means of this same poison," said Dr. Martin. "It was Lloyd George, wasn't it— some years back?"

"Yes. He was attacked by a fanatic who—"

The reception-room door was thrown open and Bullock entered, closely followed by the assistant secretary.

"'Lo, Doc," he addressed the Medical Examiner. "What's the dope?"

"A brand new one for us, Inspector. Curare!"

"Curare? Oh, my God!" cried out Bullock in mock terror. "Don't tell me it's a strange, oriental poison known only to the high priests of an obscure tribe in the upper Himalayas. Don't tell me that, 'cause I'm way behind on my Fu-Manchu stories."

The Medical Examiner smiled. He was well acquainted with the Inspector's pet phobia.

"Not oriental. It's a South American poison," he announced. "Curare is an arrow poison used by the Guarani Indians in remote parts of Paraguay and Brazil. It kills game no matter how trivial the wound may be."

Bullock groaned, but said nothing.

"Curare," continued the Medical Examiner, "also known as Urari and Woorara, is a poison which, luckily, due to difficulty in procuring, is more to be read of in medical journals than found in medical practice. In results, it somewhat resembles strychnine. Indeed the poison is derived from a species of similar weed. The poison begins its work about fifteen minutes after administration. During the first period no ill effects are observed. The symptoms consist in gradual paralysis of the respiratory muscles and death follows from asphyxia. The action of the drug is closely allied to that of cobra venom. The poison has no toxic action if taken through the mouth, provided there are no cuts or bruises in the alimentary tract or in the mucous membranes of the throat. Curare must enter into the blood stream to prove fatal."

Bullock interrupted. "Toxic action, Doc? I'm young—don't know all the big words."

"I mean the poison has to be introduced through a cut or by hypodermic injection. Drinking it won't hurt you."

"Then these two were struck with a hypo?"

"No, I didn't say that. There's a long shallow cut on the lobe of Mr. Torrent's right ear. There's also an unusual swelling in that vicinity which would ordinarily occur after a superficial injury. We can only suspect the poison entered at that spot."

"And Mr. Harrison?" queried Bullock.

The Medical Examiner spread out his hands in a gesture of resignation. "On Mr. Harrison's body there is also an area of abrasion, accompanied by a certain amount of swelling, but in his case, since the cuts could easily have become infected, it is difficult to tell whether the swelling is mild blood-poisoning, naturally following an unattended injury, or whether it is the after-results of the curare poisoning."

"Where're those cuts on Harrison?" demanded Bullock. "On his ear, too?"

"No, no. The only abrasions we can find on Mr. Harrison's body are on the left side of his face. On his upper cheek, stretching downward from just beneath the ear, are five deep scratches, quite evidently caused by the sharp points of a woman's finger nails."

4
A FEW MORE SUSPECTS

THE TELEPHONE rang.

"Well, is it tough enough for you?" demanded the Commissioner of Police when he had recognized the other's voice.

"It's a lulu!" admitted Bullock. "Both these birds got theirs at about the same time—one on the Stock Exchange, one in his office. This dame Laverne looks fishy to me but she couldn't have gotten on the Stock Exchange floor to knock off Torrent. I guess that's about the only place in the world where the fair sex has never set foot."

The Commissioner grunted into the telephone. "Didn't know there was such a place and I still doubt it."

"You find anything about Laverne?" demanded Bullock.

"Sure! We got it all—stuffing, gravy and fixings."

"A record, heh?"

"Not if you mean a police one. If you mean a bad record we might compromise by saying she has a slightly soiled one. Hemingway, that chatterbox on the *Mirror*, gave us all the dope. They've got the low-down on everybody in New York tucked away in their files. It's the liveliest morgue you ever saw. They can tell you right up to last night who was doing it to who and who paid."

"Well, what about her?" asked Bullock impatiently.

"She's been Torrent's girl, that's all."

"Well, I'll be—!" ejaculated the Inspector after a stunned interval.

"And for five years," the Commissioner elaborated.

"What did those keyhole snoopers on the *Mirror* say about her and young Harrison?"

"I asked them. They said they'd never even heard she knew him."

"Well, maybe she didn't," commented Bullock. "The people in his office said they'd never seen her before. The telephone girl said she'd never phoned him. His secretary said she'd never heard of her, although she told me Harrison had a string of fillies in his paddock that would have turned Man O' War piebald with envy."

"Did you find out where Laverne lives?"

"Sure. That was easy. At the Arden Apartments on East 62nd Street. Mulligan's cooling his heels in her front hall now. Her dinge says she doesn't know when she'll be home," said Bullock. "In the meantime you'll find me over in Torrent's office. I've got his partner Hastings waiting for me there, and afterwards I want to go through Torrent's papers."

"O. K.," answered the Commissioner. "Keep me posted."

II

TEMPLE HASTINGS sat at his desk nervously fidgeting with a pencil. In ten minutes' time this Inspector fellow—Bullet—or whatever his name was—would be seated in that chair just beside him, and he would be asked many questions about himself and Philip Torrent. His fingers shook agitatedly; petulantly he threw down his pencil. He reached into a lower drawer of his desk and brought forth a glass and a pint flask of bourbon whisky. He tossed off a stiff drink and suddenly felt better. He pushed back his chair and began to march up and down his room. From time to time he glanced impatiently at his watch. Finally he sat down once more and reopened the lower drawer.

He had just replaced the glass and bottle when there came a knock at his door.

"Inspector Bullock," announced a clerk.

Bullock rumbled into the room. As Hastings saw the heavy figure and impassive stolid face, his spirits rose. It was with an almost jaunty air that he motioned his caller to a seat.

"Well, Inspector, what can I do for you?"

Bullock gazed at the broker with speculative eyes. It was a rather strange greeting. Not at all suitable to the circumstances. Not a word of sorrow over the loss of his friend and partner—not even a mention of his name. Hastings was quite evidently flustered and most unaccountably ill at ease. The Inspector regarded the man with new interest.

"Mr. Hastings, we have to make routine investigations in cases like this among friends and relatives of the deceased," he started ponderously. "Naturally you, as Mr. Torrent's partner for many years, would be in a position to tell us more of his business affairs than anyone else."

"That is true," acknowledged the other.

The Inspector uncrossed his legs and drew his chair closer to the desk.

"Do you know of anyone who had threatened Mr. Torrent or of anyone who would benefit by his death?"

"No," replied Hastings without a moment's delay. "I do not."

"There's no possibility of blackmail or anything like that?"

"I shouldn't think so."

"His financial affairs—were they in good order?"

Hastings opened his mouth, then closed it. He thought for a moment as though to pick his words carefully.

"Mr. Torrent was a wealthy man, but naturally like all of us, he had been hurt by the events of the past four years. His estate will probably not be as large as most people imagine."

"He was on good terms with his wife?"

"Good," replied Hastings, "is a variable term. I should say he was on what I would call normal New York terms with her."

"What might that be?" demanded Bullock.

"A sort of live and let live life and the devil take the hindermost."

"And this girl—Lucy Laverne?"

"I really couldn't say a thing about that," protested Hastings. "I'm not in a position to tell you of his more personal life. It was a subject we avoided—not that I was any better in that respect," he smiled in a man-of-the-world fashion, "but I had a certain amount of reticence which kept me from prying into the matter. You must remember that I was fourteen years older than my partner and our social life, naturally, led us in different directions."

"Yeah," said Bullock, "but you must have known something about this Lucy Laverne. Were they or were they not as friendly as everyone says?"

Hastings shook his head slowly.

"I couldn't tell you that."

"Couldn't or wouldn't?" asked Bullock.

"A little bit of both. I don't see any reason why his private affairs should be bandied about."

"Nobody's bandying them," Bullock replied patiently. "After all, your partner's been murdered. A murder investigation's no Sunday-school picnic. We're interested only in facts, not morals."

Hastings put the tips of his fingers together, and he stared over them toward his questioner.

"There was a certain attachment," he finally admitted.

"Well," said Bullock, "now that you've told me what I already knew, how about telling me something I never knew before?"

He took out a cigar from his upper left waistcoat pocket, examined the tip closely and finally stuck it in the side of his mouth.

"What, for instance," he asked after scratching a match on the sole of a large shoe, "is the real low-down on Mrs. Torrent?"

"Low-down?" repeated Hastings. "I'm sure I don't know what you mean, Inspector."

Bullock took an enjoyable puff at the newly-lit cigar. His companion coughed discreetly.

"Well, then, I'll explain, Mr. Hastings. You see, you told me a little while ago that your late partner and his wife, had a 'live and let live' existence. Now I'm no Havelock Ellis but I know my way around this town enough to realize that when two people 'live and let live,' they're usually both pretty satisfied. Mr. Torrent was obviously satisfied—he had Lucy Laverne. What I want to find out is simply this—" Bullock carelessly flicked the ash of his cigar onto the carpet. "Just who was Mrs. Torrent satisfied with? That's all that's bothering me!"

"You're not suggesting Mrs. Torrent had any part in her husband's murder?" demanded Hastings incredulously.

"Not now, I'm not. But stranger things have happened. It's just an idea I'm tucking away among 'the little gray cells,' as Hercule Poirot would say."

Hastings made a gesture of annoyance. "You'd better disabuse your mind of the idea that Mrs. Torrent was connected in any fashion with her husband's murder. She happens to be a high-minded, respectable woman who would be incapable—"

"I know, I know," said Bullock gently. "A saint on earth—one of God's noblewomen."

Hastings glared at his companion angrily. "I'm not accustomed to being made mock of, Inspector," he exploded.

"Don't mind me," replied Bullock largely. "No offence meant. All my friends say I'm just full of nasty, aggravating remarks."

The broker, slightly mollified, leaned back once more in his chair.

"What else can I tell you?"

The detective's eyes smiled. He realized suddenly there was little this pompous man had told him.

"What I want now is a look through your partner's desk."

Hastings lifted his telephone receiver and gave a few instructions. A moment later the door opened and a girl stood on the threshold.

"This is Miss Snowden, Mr. Torrent's secretary. She can tell you more of my late partner's affairs than I."

Bullock glanced up at the girl's pert, intelligent face. "Yes," he said to himself, "I think she can!"

III

"What do these figures mean, Miss Snowden?"

The girl took a slip of paper from Bullock's outstretched hand and examined the writing.

STKS.	104,000
CAP.	250,000
S.E.	185,000
INS.	50,000
61st.	75,000
MIS.	19,000
C.M.	70,000
	$753,000

"I never saw this notation before," replied the girl, "but I think I understand what it is. It's a recapitulation of Mr. Torrent's worldly goods, as the storybooks say. The STKS. is stocks. I happen to know that his personal securities at the beginning of this week were valued at about that figure. The CAP. means the cash capital Mr. Torrent has in this business. The S.E. means his seat on the Exchange. The INS. is obviously insurance. 61st. is the appraised value of his house uptown. MIS. probably means miscellaneous."

She returned the paper to the detective. "They're all plain to me except the item for $70,000 marked C.M. I haven't the slightest idea what that might be."

"You're quite familiar with your late employer's business affairs?"

"I thought so," replied Miss Snowden. "I've been with the firm eight years and I've been Mr. Torrent's secretary for six. I didn't know he had anything worth $70,000 that I'd never heard of."

"Of course," pointed out Bullock judiciously, "this may have been written some years ago."

"Oh, no," denied the girl. "It was written inside of the last two days."

"How do you make that out?"

"Quite easily. The stocks, as I said, are valued on that slip of paper according to the prices which prevailed on the Stock Exchange three days ago. On that day the auditor began his usual quarterly inspection of the books. In addition there's the Stock Exchange seat at $185,000. That was the price at the last sale which took place on Monday. Previously it hadn't sold that high in ages."

Bullock grunted in approval. "You ought to be a detective, young lady. You'd be a second Madame Storey."

"Who's she?"

"Oh, just a lady dick—an old friend of mine. She knows everything and never makes a mistake."

"Then I'm afraid I don't resemble her very much," replied Miss Snowden demurely.

She showed her pretty dimples and gave the huge Inspector an arch look.

Bullock, startled, suddenly drew back into his hard-boiled shell.

"And now Miss Snowden, kindly bring me the firm's auditor. He may know something about this C.M. matter."

While the girl disappeared on her errand, Bullock sorted out of Torrent's desk a few odds and ends which he had not as yet examined. The dead broker had evidently been an extremely methodical man for there was little of the debris which usually accumulates even in the best kept desks. There were neither jotted down scraps of memoranda nor the almost inevitable litter of forgotten names, discarded addresses, and long uncalled and unwanted telephone numbers.

Torrent's business letters were neatly laid away in a battery of filing cabinets; his personal letters were non-existent.

Surely, thought Bullock, a man would have something of a personal nature in his desk. These drawers seemed so clean he had more than a suspicion they had been cleaned out by an inquisitive or acquisitive hand.

This idea had only had time to dwell in his mind for a moment when the door opened and the auditor introduced himself.

Bullock handed the man the slip of paper. “Here’s an item Miss Snowden doesn’t understand. This one—marked C.M. Can you tell me anything about it?”

The auditor glanced down the list of figures. “No,” he replied, “I can’t. It doesn’t appear on the books of the firm, although most of these other items do. It must be a personal affair—nothing connected with *Torrent & Hastings*.”

Bullock looked his disappointment.

“I’m sorry. I felt sure you could tell us something.”

The auditor shook his bald head decisively. “I can’t on that matter,” he stated, “but I can on a more important subject.”

“Well,” demanded Bullock, “and what’s that?”

The auditor did not beat about the bush. He turned a serious face toward his companion. “Inspector, you represent the police and you should know the facts. My audit has shown that Mr. Hastings is indebted to his dead partner to the amount of over three hundred thousand dollars.”

“Indebted? You mean he owes that to the Torrent estate?”

The auditor smiled grimly.

“I mean he has stolen that much!”

“When did you find this out?” asked Bullock with astonishment.

“We made certain yesterday morning.”

“Did you tell Mr. Torrent?”

“I did.”

“What did he say?”

“He was naturally very shocked. He and Mr. Hastings had been partners for years. At first he would not believe me.”

“And afterwards?” demanded Bullock.

“I don’t know what happened. Mr. Hastings was not in the office yesterday. He spent the day at his golf club; but I have reason to believe that Mr. Torrent taxed him with his dishonesty this morning before the opening of the Exchange.”

Bullock silently digested this startling piece of news.

“Mr. Hastings told me nothing of this,” he said at last.

"Naturally not," replied the auditor.

"But he must have known you would tell me. A thing like that could not be kept a secret."

"Inspector Bullock," said the auditor with an air of a schoolmaster, "you policemen are so used to cut-and-dried thievery that it is difficult for you to understand what I would call a border-line crime. A partnership, particularly a stock-exchange partnership, differs in many ways from an incorporated company. An irregularity which, in a corporation, would send it's perpetrator to jail, often, in the case of a general partnership, results in a loss to the other partners without their being able in any way to retrieve their money or even to move legally against their erring partner."

"Yeah?" observed Bullock. "Tell me some more. You sound like a senator addressing his constituents."

The auditor pointedly ignored this flippancy. He continued unperturbedly. "A partnership is what the word implies. Money one partner is personally possessed of is legally, in case of need, the property of the partnership. At law, it is almost impossible for one partner to wrong another since the two are considered to be one person.

"Now in the case of Thompkins vs. Buckley Bros., Justice Simmons of the New York Supreme Court very strongly stated that—"

"All right. We'll pass that up," interrupted Bullock. "I always believe a Judge."

The auditor did not appear to hear. His words continued to flow in a steady stream.

"Generally all partners have the right to sign the firm's name on checks. In cases of defalcation it is imperative to prove that the absconding partner used the money for his own use and not to advance the business of the firm.

"In many cases where the interests of the partnership interlock with the private affairs of the various partners it is exceedingly difficult to prove conclusively, in a case of fraud, that the accused partner actually did anything *legally* wrong.

"In the case of Mr. Hastings it will be hard—I might say almost impossible—to prove anything now that Mr. Torrent is dead. Since there were but two partners in the firm no one remains to contest Mr. Hasting's word."

Inspector Bullock had been listening to this exposition with his usual far-away look; but the last sentence jerked his stolid face into unusual animation.

"Kinda lucky, that death, for Mr. Hastings, I'd say."

The auditor inclined his head significantly. "Very," he agreed, "remarkably so."

"Where was Hastings around three o'clock this afternoon?"

His companion spread his hands in a gesture of resignation.

"You'll have to ask him that yourself," he stated, "and then check up on his answer. I wouldn't trust that man as far as I could throw him. Whatever he tells you will almost inevitably be a lie."

Bullock picked up his overcoat which was draped over a near-by chair, and placed his derby squarely and forcibly on his blunt head.

"I'll find out right now," he announced. "Thanks for your tip. I'll play it to the limit."

He walked across the reception hall, knocked at the door and entered Hastings' office.

The broker jumped up and greeted him over-effusively.

"I hope Miss Snowden could help you, Inspector?"

"Oh, yeah, she did. Nice girl, that Miss Snowden. Very fond of Mr. Torrent, too."

"Naturally, naturally. We all were," purred Hastings.

"Must have been a terrible shock to you," observed Bullock.

"Awful," assented the other. "Awful."

"Where were you when Mr. Torrent was killed?" inquired the Inspector casually.

Hastings looked up swiftly. Bullock was gazing placidly out of a near-by window.

"What did you say, Inspector?"

"I said where were you when your partner was murdered?"

"I don't know exactly what time Mr. Torrent died, but I was here in the office the whole day except for my luncheon hour."

"Where did you eat?" inquired Bullock.

"At the Stock Exchange Luncheon Club. I go there every day."

"And then you returned directly afterwards to your office?" asked the Inspector.

"Yes."

Bullock turned once more toward the door.

"I guess that'll be all, Mr. Hastings. Hope I won't have to bother you again."

He waved an arm and the door closed behind his broad shoulders.

Mr. Hastings groped toward his chair, sat down suddenly and closed his eyes.

5
FIND THE 'COMMON DENOMINATOR'

As the elevator carried him upwards, Inspector Bullock took out his fat, heavy gold watch and was surprised to find it was only five o'clock. Less than two hours had elapsed since the Commissioner had summoned him to Centre Street.

He got off at the eighth floor and walked down the long corridor to the hospital.

Dr. Martin met him in the reception room.

"Any news?" Bullock demanded.

"The Medical Examiner is in yonder. Perhaps you had better confer with him."

The Inspector entered the adjoining laboratory and found the Medical Examiner surrounded by an array of test tubes and strangely shaped retorts. "Hullo, Bullock. Made any progress?"

"A little," admitted the detective. "I've found out that Lucy Laverne was Torrent's girl friend. That ought to lead somewhere. And how about your investigation into the poisonings?"

"Our further tests have proved that the poison is the one we first suspected—curare. It found its way into Mr. Torrent's blood stream through the small cut on his right ear. In Mr. Harrison's case, it entered through the finger-nail scratches on the left side of his face."

Bullock shook his head in perplexity.

"It's a cinch both men were murdered by the same hand. What gets me is the fact they died within fifteen minutes of each other, and yet they seem to have been attacked in widely separated places.

There was no one in Harrison's office who had been on the Stock Exchange floor when Torrent first showed the results of the poison. How, then, could the same man kill young Sandy Harrison?

"When I was in high school—not that I was there very long—" continued Bullock, "I remember some sort of a thing in algebra called 'The Common Denominator.' It always gave me the willies. I never could get the idea through my head.

"As I recall, it means a number which can be divided into two other numbers. A sort of connecting link between widely separated figures. Now in these murders there must be a common denominator somewhere. Two men aren't murdered by the same person with the same poison unless there is a link *somewhere* between the three."

"Your point is well taken," said the Medical Examiner, "but I can think of several links. There's the link of Lucy Laverne—both murdered men knew her; there's the link of the Stock Exchange—they were both members. There's two of your common denominators to start off with. Finance and femininity—two pretty potent factors to worry about."

"Yes," agreed Bullock. "But I don't see much in that to help us. There's over a thousand members of the Exchange, so that denominator isn't so common; and as far as Lucy Laverne is concerned, everybody in Harrison's office says that to the best of their knowledge he had never seen or heard of her until the day of the murder."

"That's quite true," agreed the doctor with a puzzled shake of his head.

"Where's the clothes you took off the bodies?" suddenly demanded Bullock. "I'd like to look through the pockets."

"One of the nurses took the clothing away. You'll find her in the next room. She can tell you where she put them."

A few minutes later Bullock was seated before a desk sorting over two small heaps of belongings that he had taken from the pockets of the dead men's suits. Two piles of silver, two wrist watches, two pocketbooks,—the contents of the two sets of pockets were startlingly and miraculously alike. But the find which brought a sharp exclamation of amazement to his lips was discovered at almost the end of his examination.

In the breast pocket of Torrent's suit Bullock came upon a blood-spotted handkerchief. He turned it over and over and inspected it closely. It seemed as though the man had slightly cut himself while shaving and had pressed the handkerchief several times against the small cut until the bleeding had been stopped.

Automatically Bullock reached into the corresponding pocket of Harrison's suit, and withdrew another handkerchief. He looked at it dully for a moment; then put it down on the desk beside the other, and stared at the two pieces of linen with fascinated eyes. The second handkerchief was also covered with round red spots. This was similarity between the two deaths with a vengeance!

II

INSPECTOR BULLOCK and Mr. Barton seated themselves at Post 7. "It's really a misnomer to call these semi-circular enclosed spaces 'posts,'" pointed out Barton. "They're really horseshoe shaped. The name 'posts' is a hangover from before we remodeled the Exchange floor a few years ago. In those days a trading post was an upright affair with a circular bench surrounding it. Nowadays the brokers who specialize in the different stocks sit on the outside of these horseshoe trading posts while their clerks occupy the inner sides."

The head porter walked over and spread on the floor in front of the two men the contents of a burlap bag.

"This is all of it," he announced. "Everything we found within fifteen feet of this post."

It was a formidable pile of waste paper, mixed with a strange assortment of odds and ends. Bullock saw there would be a good half hour of inspection ahead of him.

He sat down on the floor; Mr. Barton, after looking with disfavor at the maneuver, finally felt himself obliged to follow suit.

"The newspapers we can discard at once," decided the Inspector. "And the scraps of ticker-tape also."

When the porters had finished removing these items there was still a compact pile waiting to be examined.

Bullock turned to the Assistant Secretary. "Mr. Barton," he said, "you know all about the order forms and printed blanks used on the Exchange. Suppose you fish out everything of that description that might interest us—everything that's written on what you might call official paper. I'll tackle the rest of this stuff."

The two set to work vigorously, and presently Bullock found before him a remarkably varied collection, which consisted of one silver-plated watch fob broken at the end; four used paper match folders marked respectively the Ha-Ha Club, the Racquet and Tennis Club, Take Bromo-Seltzer and The Warwick Hotel; one gold tie-clip; eight dunning bills (three unopened and addressed to the same man); five advertisements of a new night club; two pennies, a quarter of a dollar; six wooden pencils and one red composition metal pencil, the hollow handle filled with extra leads.

Bullock examined all these articles with meticulous care but was unable to discover among them anything that looked as though it would further his investigation.

"This is some assortment!" he commented to the head porter who was standing near by.

"Sure that ain't nothing," replied the porter. "We often collect twice that much junk. You see anything that's dropped on the floor is usually covered up right away by all this mess of waste paper that's kicked around. Every afternoon while cleaning up we find valuable personal property—jewelry and such like—that some broker has lost."

Mr. Barton, after ten minutes' silence, suddenly gave a sigh of relief. "I've finished my job, Inspector. I've sorted out everything that looks as though it might have anything to do with either Mr. Torrent or Mr. Harrison. I have set aside the following items: four buy-order slips of the firm of *Torrent & Hastings*; one discarded order slip of *Harrison & McGuire*; one scribbled memorandum addressed to Mr. Torrent and reading, 'Don't forget our luncheon engagement, J. McD.' There is also a slip of paper from the head phone-boy in the smoking room notifying Mr. Torrent he was wanted on the telephone, and another stating he was wanted at booth number 4 at the 18 Broad Street entrance. That seems to be the lot. Of course there are a great many similar pieces of paper, thrown away by other brokers, but those items would not interest you."

Bullock shook his head ponderously. "Doesn't seem to be much, but let's see what you've found." He held out his hand. "We'll start with the *Torrent & Hastings* order slips." He examined them carefully. "One reads buy 1000 IAC at the market, another buy 2500 and the third buy 500.—But why were they thrown away?" he asked Barton.

"These are the original orders, Inspector. Brought to Mr. Torrent by one of the page boys from his order phones. He bought the shares and returned his own report with the names of the brokers with whom he had traded. Then, evidently, he threw these original orders away."

"Is that customary?" asked Bullock.

"No. Most brokers keep the original orders in their pockets until after the close, but Mr. Torrent was apparently so busy in this stock that he must have absent-mindedly thrown these away."

"I see," said Bullock. "Now this order stamped with the name of the firm of *Harrison & McGuire* shows us that both Harrison and Torrent were at this post during the day. Perhaps they were both poisoned here."

"That's a pretty far-fetched idea," objected Barton. "You see International Air-Conditioning was the most active stock on the Exchange today. There would be few brokers, if any, who did not execute an order in that stock sometime during the trading hours. Naturally, Harrison, being a member of a prominent firm, was here many times with buying and selling orders. You'd have to have something more than the fact they were both at Post 7 to prove they were poisoned there."

Bullock sighed and picked up another piece of paper. "How about this luncheon date memo? Who is J. McD.?"

"I don't know, Inspector, but I think we can easily find out. Almost every member of the Exchange lunches upstairs in the Luncheon Club. The head waiter or someone will be able to tell us who Torrent was with."

"Suppose you find out for me right now who that J. McD. is," directed Bullock.

Barton scribbled a note and dispatched a porter to the Luncheon Club.

"Will the head waiter be there now?" asked Bullock. "It's after five o'clock."

"Yes," smiled Barton. "It's another one of the blessings of Repeal. This time two years ago the club was deserted after three o'clock but now the members like to linger in our new bar and lately they've even taken to ordering dinners there."

"That's a funny thing," said Inspector Bullock. "The exact same thing happened in my club, the McGillogolly Social Association of Brooklyn. Lately we've had to throw the boys out on their pants at the closing hour."

Mr. Barton's face lost its affable smile. "Oh, yes, quite," he finally managed to reply.

Bullock had not noticed the change of atmosphere.

"Now, about these telephone-call notices? Tell me about them," he demanded.

"That'll be a long story, Inspector, but this is the gist of it. Each member of the Exchange has several telephones which connect his offices to the trading floor. Over these wires come all buying and selling orders; however, under the rules of the Exchange no outside calls can be made over these private phones. They are not connected to the firm's office switchboard and therefore anyone who wants to speak directly to a member during trading hours must call him to one of the numerous telephone booths which we have in strategic places bordering the Exchange floor. One of these two printed slips which we have found addressed to Mr. Torrent is the sort used to call members to the main telephone exchange which is situated off the smoking room."

"Are there other telephone exchanges?" asked the Inspector.

"There are many phone booths scattered around but there is only one battery which has a switchboard operator. It is almost exclusively used for incoming calls. Most brokers when they wish to telephone, use one of the ordinary booths nearest to where they happen to be at the moment."

"Suppose an outside call comes to these booths—I mean the ones where there's no switchboard—what then?" demanded Bullock.

"Those phone booths are all in series of three to eight. There is always a page boy stationed outside to answer the incoming calls. He is provided with a notification pad and when a member is wanted on the phone he is sent one of these forms denoting the number and position of the booth. The second notification slip we found, addressed to Mr. Torrent, was for one of these booths—phone number 4, at the 18 Broad Street Entrance."

"I get you," announced Bullock.

He examined one of the two printed notices and read aloud, "You are wanted at telephone booth number 12 in the smoking room by Mr.—"

Bullock squinted at the signature on the bottom.

"Wanted by— I can't read that name, can you?" he demanded, handing Barton the slip with the scrawled signature at the bottom.

"The page boy who wrote this," observed the assistant secretary after he had adjusted his eyeglasses to no avail, "has not been attending our night school very assiduously. He's got the worst handwriting I ever saw. As far as I can make out the name he has written here appears to be Martini or something closely resembling it."

"A very appetizing name, too," approved Bullock. "But can we find out for sure?"

"Yes, tomorrow, when I can check up on the boy who wrote it," replied Barton. "That is, if he is able to read his own writing, which I doubt."

"It may sound of no importance to you," said the Inspector, "but usually an answer to who-were-they-with-who-were-they-talking-to-just-before-the-crime makes the difference between night and day in a murder case."

Just then the porter returned from his trip upstairs to the Luncheon Club.

He handed Barton a note from the head waiter. "Mr. Torrent lunched today with Mr. John McDonald."

"Who's McDonald?" demanded Bullock.

"He's also a member of the Exchange—a partner in *Thomkins, Jenkins & Co.*"

"Where can I find him?"

"I believe his offices are at 50 Broadway," replied Barton.

The Inspector held out his hand. "Thank you, Mr. Barton, for your assistance," he said. "You've been a great help in explaining all these technical Stock-Exchange matters. If you'll excuse me I'll drop around and see McDonald now."

The two men walked across the Exchange toward the main entrance. They stepped out into the lobby of the Stock Exchange office building and Bullock turned to bid his companion a final farewell.

Afterwards he waited until Barton had entered an elevator, then he went back to the doors of the Stock Exchange and spoke to the gray-clad special policeman who guarded the entry.

"Name of Logan, ain't it?" he demanded.

"Yes, sir," replied the guard. "I didn't think you'd remember me after all this time. It's been ten years since I was on the force."

"I've got a good memory," said Bullock, "and I hope you have."

"Try me, Inspector," the man demanded.

"All right," challenged Bullock. "Do you know Mr. Temple Hastings?"

"The partner of the man who was murdered— I'll say I do."

"Have you seen him lately?"

"Why sure," asserted Logan. "Although he doesn't come past me very often I did see him today. Only this afternoon he came down from the Luncheon Club and went onto the Exchange floor."

"At what time?" demanded Bullock eagerly.

"I couldn't tell you to the minute, Inspector, but I'd say it was somewhere around two thirty or perhaps a little later—possibly fifteen minutes before the Exchange closed."

6

WHAT THE WAITER HEARD

BULLOCK RECEIVED this piece of information with complete equanimity.

"I had a hunch I might find out something like that," he said to himself, "although I did think I'd have to inquire at more than one entrance."

He waved a friendly arm toward the guard, and hurried across the lobby to catch an elevator that was closing its doors.

At the Luncheon Club floor he asked for the head waiter and a moment later the two men were sitting in a corner of the deserted lounge.

"Yes, Inspector," the head waiter replied, "Mr. Torrent and Mr. McDonald lunched together. I remember seeing them myself. They lingered a very long time over their lunch—almost an hour, which is unusual on busy days like these."

"They must have been having a pretty important discussion, I should say," observed Bullock. "They'd hardly be wasting their valuable time, otherwise."

The head waiter nodded his assent. "I don't know if it was an important discussion or not, but it was a heated one."

"Oh, yeah?" demanded the Inspector. "How'd you make that out?"

"They were both mad as hornets about something. Once Mr. Torrent banged the table so hard with his fist that he knocked a water glass to the floor. Their waiter, Jules, came and told me about it at the time. He was afraid he would be charged for the breakage."

"That's interesting," said Bullock. "Did it look to you as though they were mad at each other or mutually mad *about* something?"

The head waiter chuckled genially. "That's a stiff one, Inspector. Too hard for me to answer. I'm afraid I'm not detective enough or didn't watch them closely enough to give you much of an opinion."

Bullock nodded gloomily. "How about their waiter? Is he here now? He could probably tell us something. I never saw a waiter yet whose ears weren't flapping."

"Jules isn't here now," replied the head waiter. "Most of our waiters leave after lunch. Many of them have other jobs for dinner and supper, but I can find out where the man you want can be found and I'll ask him anything you wish."

"Fine," said Bullock. "You ask him if he heard what Torrent and McDonald were talking about. I'll call you later for news."

He inquired where the head waiter could be reached in the evening and bade him a cheerful goodbye. As he left the Stock Exchange, Bullock's spirits were considerably higher. Things were coming along a little quicker than he had anticipated.

As he walked up Wall Street he glanced at the clock on Trinity Church steeple. Six o'clock. Too late now to find McDonald at his offices. Better to interview Mrs. Torrent.

He dived down the subway steps and caught an uptown express. Changing to a local at Grand Central he emerged finally into the bustle of 59th and Lexington Avenue. He elbowed his way through the late shopping crowds and a few minutes' walk brought him in front of Torrent's home—a white granite, five-story building bedecked with flowering window boxes.

He walked up to the ornately grilled doorway and pushed the doorbell.

The ring was answered by a severe-looking butler who appeared not at all surprised by the visit. He took Bullock's coat and hat and ceremoniously led the way upstairs to a cozy sitting room on the second floor.

Excusing himself, the man withdrew and returned a minute later to inform the Inspector that Mrs. Torrent would join him shortly.

Left to himself Bullock sauntered around the room. He examined with interest the two Corot's that hung on either side of the red marble mantel, and he fingered with appropriate respect the *petit-point* of the Queen Anne chairs. Not very often did his official or unofficial duties lead him into such elaborately and beautifully furnished residences.

Presently he heard footsteps in the corridor and Mrs. Torrent entered the room. She greeted Bullock graciously and seated herself near the fireplace.

The Inspector regarded her gravely. She was a younger woman than he had expected—thirty-eight or so he hazarded. In any event she was many years' junior to her elderly husband. The slim, rounded figure, the pink and white complexion of her face and arms, proclaimed her a girl still in her teens; but the sophisticatedly coiffured hair and the calm insolence of her blue eyes were those of a mature and self-possessed woman.

There were no signs of sorrow, recent or present, to mar the smoothness of her face, nor was there even a hint of tremor in her voice when she spoke. For a widow of but a few hours, she seemed to be carrying her sorrow easily.

"You wish to question me, Inspector?"

Bullock inclined his head. "Just a few formalities, Mrs. Torrent."

She sat expectantly waiting.

"Do you know of anyone who had cause to kill your husband?"

Mary Torrent shook her head decisively. "No one. My husband, like most successful men in Wall Street, had incurred the enmity of other brokers in the course of business deals, but I hardly think any of these men could be suspected of murder."

"The fact remains, Mrs. Torrent, that somebody hated your husband sufficiently to do that very thing."

Bullock sat silent for a moment. "Is there no one who would benefit by his death?" he asked.

"That's a silly question, Inspector. Someone always benefits by any man's death. It would be ridiculous to contend otherwise. I don't know the exact terms of my husband's will, but I presume there are others beside myself who will benefit financially. For instance, young Howard Torrent, my husband's nephew, will come into the sole control of his father's estate, and will also inherit a considerable trust fund left to my husband by his late brother. Philip had what I believe is called a life-tenancy in the income derived from a large apartment building on Fifth Avenue. This will now go to Howard Torrent."

"This Howard—what sort of a boy is he?"

"He is a drunken, dissolute, ungrateful and thoroughly disagreeable youth. My husband spent the last ten years getting him out of one disgraceful escapade after another. He was dropped from two schools, expelled from Harvard, and during the last three years has been sued twice for breach of promise."

"I take it there was no love lost between your husband and his nephew?"

"Mr. Torrent felt sorry for the boy and was disgusted by his actions. I am sure that was the extent of his feelings. As to Howard I am afraid his reactions were of a more violent sort. He hated my husband in an unreasonable and unreasoning manner, and he often made threats against Mr. Torrent."

"Threats?" demanded the Inspector. "What kind of threats?"

"I don't know. My husband never told me what they were, but I know that he was very much upset by them."

"Threats of death, perhaps?"

"No, Mr. Torrent would have laughed away anything like that. He wasn't a person who could be easily intimidated or frightened."

Bullock shifted uneasily about in his chair, lunged his huge shoulders forward and clasped his hands nervously. Taking a deep breath, he plunged.

"Mrs. Torrent, were you happy with your husband?"

Mary Torrent laughed musically. "Really, Inspector, you are positively old-fashioned. What do you mean—happy?"

Bullock blushed and looked exceedingly uncomfortable.

"I mean—I mean—" he stammered, "I've heard that—"

Mary Torrent cut him short. The smile had gone out of her voice.

"You mean you've heard my husband was keeping a woman. Isn't that what you wish to say?"

The Inspector, vastly relieved, nodded eagerly. "That's about what I was getting at."

"You needn't have been so embarrassed," declared Mrs. Torrent. "Adding to their collection of girls is a habit rich brokers have—seems to run in their blood. It isn't considered quite *comme il faut* on the Stock Exchange to have only a legalized establishment. A successful broker is known more by the companies he keeps than by those he floats. Fortunately, my husband was intelligent enough to escape the vicissitudes of the depression years; therefore his escutcheon, in regard to his obligations toward his little friends, was quite unsullied. He emerged from the financial chaos still a perfect gentleman."

Bullock coughed apologetically. "Then you were aware of his attachment to Miss Laverne?"

"Yes," replied Mary Torrent. "She was the last of a long series. The most attractive, I believe, also. She was pointed out to me some months back, and I must say I always approved of Philip's taste in women. At least, I was never insulted by unattractive competition."

Bullock appeared quite satisfied to let the subject drop. He continued in a different vein. "In looking over Mr. Torrent's papers, we have come upon an item marked C.M. which apparently is either the name of some sort of property or the name of somebody who owes your husband seventy thousand dollars. That is a large sum of money and no one in his office seems to know a thing about it. Do you?"

"No," replied Mrs. Torrent. "My husband never mentioned financial affairs in his home. He had the happy faculty, unusual in brokers, of being able to leave his business at his office."

"How well do you know Mr. Hastings, your husband's partner?"

"I know him, but that is about all. His wife is a type of woman I cannot abide; consequently I made arrangements to see as little of them as possible."

"What were your husband's relations with his partner?"

"Excellent, I believe. They had been together for many years. Philip had great regard for Mr. Hastings' business ability, and often used to say he didn't know what he would do without him."

"It's unfortunate he placed so much confidence in him," stated the Inspector bluntly.

Mary Torrent looked questioningly at Bullock. "Just what do you mean?"

"Your husband was robbed by his partner of a great sum of money; exactly how much cannot be determined until a thorough audit is made. Whatever the amount proves to be it will be large enough to seriously damage the value of Mr. Torrent's estate. That is also one of the reasons we are so anxious to discover what the initials of C.M. stand for—and where the missing seventy thousand dollars can be located."

Mrs. Torrent remained silent for a moment, then slowly and decisively shook her head. "I'm sorry, Inspector. I repeat I cannot help you. I know nothing about the matter. As I told you I had—"

The butler came quietly into the room and crossed over toward the fireplace.

"Mr. McDonald is calling, Madam."

Bullock's impassive face was very nearly brought to life by this simple announcement. He glanced quickly at Mrs. Torrent.

There was a look of fright in her blue eyes. She nervously wetted her lips with the tip of her tongue and stared with ill-concealed apprehension over the butler's shoulder toward the doorway.

"Tell Mr. McDonald I am busy for the present. Ask him to call later."

Bullock raised his hand in hasty protestation. "Mrs. Torrent, I have no more questions to ask you. By all means don't let me send your friend away. I was just about to leave, anyhow."

"Very well, then," she motioned to the butler, "show Mr. McDonald in."

She waited until the man had left the room, then turned once more to the Inspector. "Mr. McDonald was one of my husband's friends."

"I see," said Bullock politely.

A moment later the caller crossed the threshold.

He was a lean, sallow, good-looking man, with the dark sleek assurance of an aging movie star. He moved across the room and took Mary Torrent's two hands in his.

"I'm so sorry," he whispered.

Was it Bullock's imagination or did the woman recoil from McDonald's touch as he said the conventional words of sympathy? In any event, she quickly drew back into her chair and introduced the Inspector. "This is Inspector Bullock of the Police Department."

McDonald took the Inspector's proffered hand and shook it warmly.

"I certainly hope you'll quickly solve these dreadful affairs. It's been a great shock to all of us on the Exchange. One could hardly have picked in the whole of New York two more genial and popular men than Sandy Harrison and Philip Torrent. I declare the whole thing—even now—seems to be only a fantastic, terrible dream."

Bullock nodded in agreement. "It must be a great blow to their friends. You, I understand, were particularly friendly with Philip Torrent?"

He paused and looked at Mary Torrent. She was staring into the flickering flames of the hearth.

"Yes," replied the broker. "We have been friends for many years."

Acting on a sudden hunch, Bullock decided it was time for him to leave. This was not the time nor the place to ask McDonald about the strangely tense luncheon hour.

Accordingly he rose and bade Mrs. Torrent and McDonald goodbye; a minute later the solemnfaced butler had ushered him through the outer doors.

At the corner of Madison Avenue he entered a cigar store and dialed the number which the head waiter at the Luncheon Club had given him.

"This is Inspector Bullock," he stated when a voice answered. "Did you get in touch with Jules, the waiter?"

The head waiter's voice rose in excitement; his voice screeched into the receiver at Bullock's ear.

"I'll say I have—Listen! Jules said he only heard a bit of their conversation but that bit was hot enough to make him want to hear more. Unfortunately he said they got up and left the table just as he was getting an earful."

"Well, what was it?" demanded Bullock, who did not approve of the head waiter's verbosity.

"Just this," continued the other. "According to the waiter, McDonald and Torrent were having a terrible argument. The word divorce was mentioned two or three times, and the last thing he heard before the men left their table was Torrent cursing McDonald at the top of his voice."

"Exactly what did he say?" demanded Bullock eagerly.

"Torrent's last words before he left the table," answered the head waiter, "were, 'I'll see you in hell first.'"

"Humph," said Bullock as he replaced the telephone receiver on its hook, "just a couple of old pals!"

7
A BOTTLE OF BRAZILIAN BURNISH

MEANWHILE THE PATIENT Mulligan still held his lonely vigil on the long, teakwood bench that stood in the entrance-way of Lucy Laverne's apartment.

Hours had passed and there was still no sign of the missing girl. Finally, when it was well after eleven o'clock, the colored maid began to show anxiety.

"Ah sure think there's sumptin' mighty strange," she announced. "Look here, Mister Detective, this ain't like Miss Lucy, no, it ain't. I allows she keeps what some folks call irregularity hours, but when she ain't comin' home to dinner she allus calls up, yas suh."

Just then the doorbell pealed. Mulligan jumped to his feet. "Here she is now."

The maid sniffed. "Does yo' ring yo' doorbell when yo' gits home?"

With this Parthian shot she paraded down the hallway with a great air of dignity. She opened the door with a flourish. On the threshold stood Inspector Bullock.

"Hello, Mulligan," he said, as he gave the maid his hat and coat. "I've come to take your place for a while. Guess you must be hungry. Go get your dinner; telephone me here in three hours. If Miss Laverne hasn't returned you'll have to come back and rest your weary bones on this settee again."

Mulligan left in haste to search for his lost meal. Bullock settled himself in the most comfortable chair in Lucy Laverne's sitting room and picked out a detective novel from a nearby bookcase. He turned to the first page and soon was deeply absorbed in the gory details of the murder of a prime minister and his entire cabinet.

When the Inspector was halfway through page 64 (where the minister of agriculture was about to be shot), he heard the elevator clang open and a moment later a key was inserted in the door of the apartment.

The maid hurried out of the kitchen and rushed down the hall. He heard a swift exchange of sibilant whispers; then Lucy Laverne entered the sitting room.

Bullock rose to his feet. "Miss Laverne?"

"Naturally."

The Inspector coughed apologetically. "Miss Laverne, we've been waiting for you for the last five hours. I was beginning to think you were never coming back."

"And if I hadn't, what business would it have been of yours?" she demanded.

The Inspector suddenly lost most of his affable manner. His bushy eyebrows came together in a portentous frown. "Miss Laverne, you'll get nowhere taking that attitude. You realize—or at least you ought to realize—the reason for our interest in you. Your relations with Philip Torrent were well known among his friends and associates. You can hardly pretend that we wouldn't question you after his murder?"

"I don't know a thing about it," she replied. "I'm sure I can be of no assistance to you."

"That," declared Bullock, "remains to be seen. Personally I think you can do a great deal to help us."

He sat back in his chair and his masculine eyes took in with complete approval the face and figure of the girl who sat nervously facing him.

Short black hair, cut in Buster Brown fashion, contrasted vividly with the blue of her eyes and the crimson of her lips; a pert little nose plus a round determined chin added to the attractiveness of the picture.

Lucy Laverne, despite her Gallic name, was quite evidently Irish. Needless to say this was not calculated to decrease Bullock's interest.

"Miss Laverne," the Inspector continued, "I have a number of questions to ask you. We will start with the one I think is the most important. And that is—who do you think killed Philip Torrent?"

"I don't know," she replied decisively. "There's many people who disliked Philip Torrent, but as for murder—it takes more than a dislike for that."

"Quite so," agreed Bullock. "And now for question number two— What do you know about Sandy Harrison's private affairs?"

The girl shook her head. "I hardly knew Sandy. In fact I met him for the first time at a cocktail party yesterday. He was a very young and very affable young man and was, I understand, most popular with everyone. I can't conceive of a person hating him to the extent of murder."

"Question number three," went on the Inspector. "When did you see Philip Torrent last?"

"I lunched with him yesterday."

"Would it be too much to ask what transpired at that luncheon—if there was anything he told you that might possibly have a bearing on his death?"

Lucy Laverne faced her questioner bravely, but there were tears in her eyes when she finally answered.

"Mr. Torrent said his wife was trying to divorce him. He also told me our friendship was at an end."

"He gave you reasons for his wife's decision?"

"No."

"Didn't he say she wanted to marry someone else?"

"No," repeated Lucy Laverne, "but that usually follows, doesn't it?"

Bullock ignored the question. "Now, Miss Laverne, what can you tell me about Mr. Sandy Harrison? Although you say you hardly were acquainted, I understand that he was on intimate terms with many of your friends. That's right, isn't it?"

"He went around a lot with a girl I know," she admitted. "But as for myself I was only with him twice in my life, this afternoon and last night."

The Inspector showed his surprise. "You say you were with him last night?" he demanded.

"Why, yes—I thought I'd mentioned it. I had dinner with him. Afterwards we went dancing."

Bullock regarded the girl with amazement. "My dear young woman," he said at last, "do you realize what you're saying?"

"I don't know what you mean."

"I'll explain," he answered. "Mr. Philip Torrent, a friend of yours, and Mr. Sandy Harrison, also your friend, were murdered this morning on the Stock Exchange. Yesterday you lunched with Torrent and dined with Harrison; then, this afternoon, you were with Harrison when he was poisoned."

The girl gazed at Bullock with horror-stricken eyes; she wet her lips with the tip of her tongue, started to reply, thought better of it, and remained silent.

"Lot of coincidence there, eh?" demanded the policeman. "I don't suppose you saw Mr. Torrent today also?"

There was a long silence; finally he repeated his query.

"Yes," she admitted, "I did."

"And when was that?" demanded Bullock, astounded that this chance question had borne such a result.

"This afternoon—just before the closing. I stopped at the Exchange and sent in for him. He met me in the 11 Wall Street lobby."

"What did you want to see him about?" demanded Bullock bluntly.

The girl hung her head, took out a small handkerchief from her purse and dabbed ineffectually at her eyes.

'I was determined to make one more appeal, even though I knew it was a silly thing to do."

"You went all the way downtown for that purpose?"

"No. I did it on the spur of the moment. I'd been to my dentist—his offices are in that neighborhood."

"What did Mr. Torrent say to you?"

"He was very angry. He told me he was too busy to talk—that it was very embarrassing to have me there."

She hastily used her handkerchief again. "As a matter of fact," she sobbed, "he told me quite definitely he didn't want me to bother him any more."

The Inspector waited for a few minutes until the girl had gotten herself under better control, then proceeded with his next question. "That explains your visit to Torrent, but why did you call on Harrison?"

"Because I was so angry at Philip. It was just a little while before the Exchange closed so I went to Sandy's office to wait for him."

"And what happened when Harrison arrived?"

"I apologized for being mean to him the night before."

"Mean?" queried Bullock. "How?"

"We were in a night club; we had an argument; I scratched his face."

"What for?"

"I don't know. We were both tight. Philip had given me the air—I didn't care what happened. That's the only reason I went out with Sandy."

"And so you called at Mr. Harrison's office to apologize for scratching his face?"

"Yes."

"There was no other reason?"

"No."

Bullock had a very serious expression on his face when he asked the next question.

"What happened in Harrison's office?"

"I waited for about fifteen or twenty minutes; then he arrived and took me into his private office. I told him how sorry I was; he said everything was all right and to forget the whole affair. Then we started to talk on some inconsequential subject. We had chatted for only a few minutes when he leapt up from his chair with a most dreadful look on his face, gasped and fell to the floor. I screamed, several clerks rushed in and then the stretcher bearers came and carried him down to the hospital. I tried to go with them but they wouldn't let me. I argued and argued but it didn't do any good. Finally I went uptown to a friend's apartment; while there I telephoned to the Stock Exchange hospital and they told me Sandy was dead!"

"And then what?" urged Bullock.

"That was horrible enough," continued the girl, "but later in the afternoon, while I was still at Helen's apartment, the evening papers were delivered and I read that Philip had also died."

She covered her face with her hands. "Oh, it was too awful! The two men I had seen that very afternoon—both murdered!"

"I can quite sympathize with you," said Bullock. "But when young Harrison was stricken in that most peculiar manner, you should have stayed in his office and waited for the police or the hospital authorities to question you."

"Just why?" she demanded with a return of spirit. "I thought he'd had a stroke or something like that. Why should I dream there'd be any police mixed up in the affair?"

The Inspector considered the reply for a moment, then nodded his agreement. "Quite true. I hadn't thought of it that way."

He reached across the small space that separated him from the girl. "May I see your fingers?" he asked.

Lucy Laverne looked at the detective with amazement; seeing he was not jesting, but grimly in earnest, she gave him her hands.

"Where do you have your nails manicured?" Bullock asked.

"At Pedro's on East 58th Street."

"When were they done last?"

"A week or so ago."

"They appear remarkably well cared for. Sure it wasn't later than that?"

"No; but I polish them myself every morning."

"With one of Pedro's polishes?"

"Yes. It's the best polish I've ever used. It's called Brazilian Burnish."

The Inspector sat back suddenly. "South American—this Pedro?" he demanded.

"Why, yes. He has a wonderful beauty shop. One of the best in New York. Surely you've heard of him."

"A little out of my line," Bullock explained. "You say he's the proprietor of a very popular hairdressing and manicuring establishment."

"Divine," proclaimed Lucy Laverne. "He does the most marvelous marcelle and as for his nail polishes— I don't know which I like best, the Brazilian Burnish I'm using now or the Paraguayan Polish or the—"

Bullock raised his hand in mock dismay. "That's all of South America I want to travel through right now," he announced. "But what I'd like to know is—have you a bottle of this divine Brazilian Burnish?"

"Why, yes," she replied wonderingly.

"I'd like to see it."

The girl got up without another word and went into the adjoining bedroom. She returned with a small red bottle.

"Thanks," said Bullock. "I'll borrow this."

"But I need it," she remonstrated.

"I need it the most," he replied. "My nails are in the most frightful state."

The two laughed together. "But," he promised her, "I'll return it tomorrow."

Bullock hunched his huge shoulders forward and pointed a finger at the girl who sat facing him. "Miss Laverne, I don't mind telling you, you're in a tough spot. There's plenty of flat-feet down at Headquarters that'd be pulling you in for murder right this second. You had lunch yesterday with Torrent and dinner with Harrison. Today you saw Torrent a few minutes before he died and you were with Harrison when he was poisoned—or, at the very least, when the poison took effect. Sort of a long train of circumstances, I'd say. And on top of that you'd just been given the air by your friend Torrent, and certainly if I know anything about women they consider that as good a ground for murder as anything I ever heard of."

Now that a real accusation had been thrown at her, Lucy Laverne's Irish blood came boiling up. "That's perfectly ridiculous. Why in heaven's name would I murder Sandy Harrison?"

"I don't know," frankly admitted Bullock. "But I might give a good guess if you told me why you scratched his face."

"Don't be silly," she exclaimed. "You're trying to frighten me."

"On the contrary, I'm trying to show you the seriousness of your present position."

Lucy smiled with new assurance. She was beginning to like this great hulk of a man.

"And then will you please tell me why I would want to murder Philip Torrent?" she continued. "He had promised me a financial settlement of generous proportions. Surely I wouldn't kill the goose that laid the golden eggs, particularly before I had received the eggs?"

"A woman scorned—" began Bullock.

"Rot!" she interrupted. "That was in old-fashioned story-books. Nowadays pretty women don't stay scorned very long. I'll admit I was in a rage when Philip told me our affair was ended, but by late afternoon I had decided that perhaps our break was all for the best. As he told me himself it would have been inevitable some day."

Bullock slipped the bottle of nail polish into his jacket pocket. He stood up and held out his hand with a friendly gesture. "Miss Laverne, after hearing your explanation, I don't believe you had anything to do with these murders; however, I must ask you not to leave the city until further notice."

A minute later he stepped out of the elevator on the ground floor. He looked at his watch. It was after one o'clock, but there was still work to be done. He walked the few blocks to the nearest precinct station house, entered the dingy building and greeted the desk sergeant cheerily.

"Wake up, you old so and so. Have you got a man you can spare?"

Sergeant Muldoon grinned. "For you, Inspector," he announced largely, "we'll wake up all the reserves."

"One man's all I need," said Bullock. He took the bottle of Brazilian Burnish from his pocket and wrapped it in a newspaper provided by a sleepy policeman, who had been summoned from upstairs.

"To the Medical Examiner's office," he directed the man. "He's gone home, of course, at this hour, but perhaps some of his smart young men may be sitting there wrapping themselves around a quart of rye."

He scribbled a hasty note. "Anyhow, deliver this package and letter."

Bullock went behind the Sergeant's desk and perched himself precariously on its lofty side. With his friend, Sergeant Muldoon, he spent a very pleasant half hour reminiscing the happy, old days when they had tramped the pavements together.

Suddenly he remembered Mulligan. He picked up the telephone on the Sergeant's desk, and soon was connected with the detective's home.

"Say, Inspector," were Mulligan's first words. "The Commissioner just called me to find out if I knew where you were. He wants you to phone him at his home."

"O.K. I'll call him right away," Bullock answered.

"Want me any more?" inquired Mulligan.

"No. You can go to bed. I don't think the situation we were looking into is very serious."

He hung up, then telephoned the Commissioner at his residence. Mackay was evidently very much awake for no sooner had the servant taken Bullock's name than Mackay was on the phone. "Who's this?" demanded the Commissioner. "Bullock, eh? Fine! Just want to tell you something. Mrs. Torrent called. She said she was sure you'd be interested. They read Philip Torrent's will an hour or so ago—and it makes mighty good reading."

"Well?"

"She tells me that Torrent left Lucy Laverne fifty thousand dollars."

"Whew!" whistled the Inspector. "I'll be damned!"

The Commissioner continued. "I'm giving you this for what it's worth. It may mean nothing and it may mean much."

"I'll attend to it, Chief," said Bullock ringing off. Hastily he dialed a telephone number. "That you, Mulligan? Your troubles aren't over. Go back to the Alden Apartments, sit downstairs in the lobby and if that girl goes out tonight you stick to her tighter than a chorus girl's brassiere."

8
THE CLUE OF THE RED METAL PENCIL

AT NINE O'CLOCK next morning Bullock arrived at the grim, grimy old building on Centre Street, and scorning a rickety elevator ascended the broad staircase to the offices of the Police Commissioner.

He nodded to the uniformed policeman who guarded the sacred portals and entered the great square room. John Mackay, puffing on his inevitable long cigar, sat behind the desk dictating furiously to a stenographer.

"Well, Inspector," he demanded, "any more progress?"

"Not yet," admitted Bullock. "Barton, down at the Exchange, is still trying to find out which one of the page boys wrote the name of the caller on the telephone slip addressed to Torrent—the name that looks like Martini—remember?"

John Mackay nodded in reply.

"Of course, Barton couldn't check up yesterday," continued Bullock, "because most of the page boys had gone for the day; but he told me this morning there's no possibility of his not identifying the boy. It's only a question of time. And then as for Lucy Laverne, the man that relieved Mulligan called me a little while ago. She hasn't come out of her apartment yet."

The telephone on the desk between the two men rang imperiously. Mackay leaned over and picked up the receiver. "Yes, he's here." He handed the instrument to Bullock. "Speaking of the devil, it's your friend Barton."

The Inspector listened to Barton, said, "Yeah," and hung up.

He turned to the Police Commissioner. "He's found the page boy."

"Fine," said Mackay. "And then what?"

"The name of the person who called Torrent was not Martini—but Marinelli."

"And so the boy could read his own handwriting after all," observed Mackay with a smile.

"Seems so," assented Bullock. "He also told Barton that he remembers Marinelli's first name although he didn't put it on the telephone slip. He remembers the Christian name because it was such an unusual one."

"Well," demanded the Commissioner of Police, "what was it?"

"Chipo."

"Chipo Marinelli," ejaculated Mackay, suddenly interested. "Why in the world would a fellow like that be telephoning Philip Torrent?"

"You know him?" queried Bullock. "A crook, eh?"

"Not exactly. He runs a speak-easy up on 51st Street. Been there six or seven years, but the Alcoholic Beverage Control Board wouldn't give him a license when liquor came in."

"Wouldn't give him a license!" It was now Bullock's turn to be surprised. "You don't mean to tell me there's a single speak-easy in town that those birds wouldn't license? What have they got against him—murder?"

"Almost," admitted his superior. "He was mixed up in a nasty shooting last year. It's never been explained to our satisfaction. In addition, he has a sweet number of arrests that don't help his record any—although they're mostly, I believe, for petty offences."

The Commissioner pushed an electric button and a staff sergeant appeared.

"Get me the dossier of a Chipo Marinelli—runs a speak-easy on 51st Street."

The sergeant saluted and left the room. He returned shortly with the desired records.

The Commissioner rapidly glanced down the sheets of paper. "Like most of them," he commented sourly. "Pulled in twenty times—never convicted. First arrested in 1918 and eight times more in the past six years."

A stubby finger followed the list of items down the page and stopped at the last entry. He whistled in surprise and pointed out the line to Bullock. "Last arrested only yesterday. On the complaint of the district leader. Seems the restaurants in the neighborhood were sore because Marinelli was allowed to stay in business without a license."

"What happened to him?" inquired the Inspector.

"Out on bail supplied by his lawyer."

"Maybe he phoned Torrent to get bail for him," suggested Bullock.

"Possibly," said Mackay. "That's an angle we can look into, but he'll tell us why he called Torrent all right or I'll know the reason why. Thank God the hey-hey days of these hoodlums are over as far as we're concerned." The Commissioner glared fiercely at Bullock, and demanded, "You told me last night about some odds and ends you collected on the Exchange floor. Have you brought them with you, Inspector?"

"Yep," replied Bullock, "right here—" He pulled up an attaché case and laid it in front of the Commissioner.

"It's a mess of nothing, I'd say, but here it is for you to look at."

Mackay opened up the bag and put on the desk the mixed assortment of articles—the watch fob, the match folders, the gold tie-clip, the unpaid bills, the night club advertisements, the six wooden pencils and the one composition pencil.

"You can see, Chief," observed Bullock, "that even Sherlock Holmes would have a time finding out anything from this junk."

The Commissioner grunted in agreement. "I wouldn't call you a liar. The whole collection looks sort of slim as far as clues are concerned. A lot of damn advertisements, bills and pencils—" He pushed the exhibits aside with a gesture of derision. "Let's forget about these so-called clues and get down to personalities. From what you tell me we have plenty of them to worry about."

The Commissioner of Police drew a clean piece of paper out of an upper drawer in his desk and reached in front of him for a pencil. "First," he said, "we have Hastings who seems to be worth thinking about. We'll put him down at the head of our list of suspects."

Mackay picked up the pencil and started to write the word "Hastings."

Instead of leaving a pencil mark the lead tore a long jagged hole in the letter paper. Surprised, the Commissioner tried again with precisely the same result. He took up the pencil and examined it more closely. It was the composition pencil that Bullock had found on the Stock Exchange floor. He turned it over in his hand; to all appearances it was an ordinary pencil. Why, then, wouldn't it write? He pulled off the cap underneath the eraser and a dozen unused leads came tumbling out. He drew several of them one by one across a sheet of paper and found that there was nothing wrong with any of these points. He examined the offending pencil point again—felt it with his finger, pressed it once more against the paper.

Bullock sat watching with amazement. He could make neither head nor tail out of his superior's actions. "What's the big idea?" he finally demanded, his curiosity outweighing the strictness of official decorum.

The Commissioner twisted the screw bottom of the pencil and the point fell out. He touched it gingerly as it lay on the blotter before him.

"What sort of hocus-pocus is this?" he demanded. "Do you see what I see?"

Bullock leaned over his superior's shoulder and gazed at the small dark object.

"Well, I'll be damned," he ejaculated. "It's a phonograph needle."

"It most certainly is," replied Mackay, "and it's covered with some sort of black stuff. Maybe it's curare poison?" He looked ruefully at his fingers. "I certainly hope not after all the handling I've been giving this pencil."

"Don't worry about that," consoled Bullock. "The Medical Examiner told me the poison can only enter through a cut."

The Commissioner opened a drawer and drew out a white envelope. In this he carefully placed the phonograph needle, scribbled a few words on a piece of paper and dispatched the letter by a policeman with instructions to deliver it immediately to the Medical Examiner's office.

"I've told Dr. Moss to analyze the black material which covers the phonograph needle. He'll naturally do it as quickly as possible, but you know how these doctors are. He'll probably fuss and fume, and check and recheck his findings for a couple of hours, and like as not we won't hear from him until this afternoon."

"That's all right by me," said Bullock. "I think I can spend a couple of hours down at the Exchange to good advantage. If you want to get hold of me you can call Barton's office and leave a message."

II

BULLOCK ARRIVED at the Stock Exchange just in time to prevent Barton from leisurely enjoying his midday meal. The assistant secretary, in answer to the urgent message, had to leave his luncheon untouched and hurry downstairs to his office where the Inspector was waiting impatiently.

"I want to go on the Stock Exchange floor. Now, during trading hours," said Bullock. "I don't know whether it's ever been permitted by non-members, but there are some investigations I must make while the play is on, so to speak."

"It's not usual," replied Barton, "but under the circumstances I think we can quickly arrange for permission—if you'll excuse me for a moment I'll speak to the secretary."

He returned a few minutes later with the information that Bullock had been given *carte blanche* to visit any part of the building he desired.

"I've been delegated to show you around," Barton told him as they descended to the trading floor, "and I think the best way for you to get a comprehensive idea of the workings of the Exchange would be to follow a broker around the floor and watch him as he executes his usual flow of orders which will take him to all parts of the Exchange floor." With Barton showing the way, they walked across the Exchange. It was now a far different place from the deserted and silent room of the previous afternoon. A babble of raucous shouts, blended together, made a constant monotonous roar, that neither changed its tone nor volume.

The Inspector took his guide's arm and shouted into his ear, "I want to go to Post 7 first. There's a few little matters that need looking into there." The two men shouldered past hurrying brokers who miraculously seemed to be endowed with some sixth sense that enabled them to escape violent head-on collisions with fellow Stock Exchange members.

At the International Air-Conditioning post there was not as much excitement as on the previous day, but there was still enough activity and strength in the stock to make it a satisfactory day for both brokers and their customers.

Barton introduced the Inspector to several brokers who were sitting on the small leather seats that jutted out from the sides of the horseshoe-shaped trading post.

The assistant secretary essayed a feeble joke. "You see," he pointed out to Bullock, "we have seats on the Stock Exchange—notwithstanding rumors to the contrary. But I will admit they're pretty small and uncomfortable affairs considering the price you have to pay to sit on them."

Bullock, smiling absently at the joke which he felt sure must be of a very ancient vintage, drew out of his pocket the red metal pencil and showed it to the little knot of brokers surrounding him.

"Any of you gentlemen ever see this before?" he demanded. One by one the brokers examined the pencil; all denied ever having seen it previously.

Finally he took the pencil to the space inside the broad ends of the trading post where seven or eight clerks were making entries in the specialists' order books.

The second clerk he showed it to recognized the pencil at once.

"Sure. I remember this. Let's see—it belonged to one of the boys. I saw it yesterday or the day before."

"What do you mean one of the boys?" asked Bullock. "Do you mean one of your fellow clerks?"

The clerk did not appear to hear the question. He was scratching his head in perplexity.

"I've got it," he announced. "That's Torrent's pencil."

Bullock's jaw dropped wide open.

"Torrent," he repeated, goggle-eyed. "You mean Mr. Torrent who was murdered?"

"Naw," replied the other. "I mean one of the clerks that works here with us. His name's Torrent

too."

"Where is he?" demanded the Inspector.

"Out to lunch. He'll be back soon."

While he waited for the clerk's return, Bullock found it almost impossible to control his impatience. He walked back and forth across the Exchange in a vain attempt to make the minutes go more swiftly. Barton at his side kept pointing out and explaining various features of the mechanics of stock trading, but the Inspector hardly bothered to listen. Finally they went back to Post 7 and found that Torrent had returned.

"Is this your pencil?" the Inspector demanded without preliminaries. The clerk looked at the pencil for a moment. "I think so," he admitted. "I had one like it for a couple of weeks."

"What happened to it?"

Torrent shrugged his shoulders. "Search me. Lost it or somebody borrowed it, I guess. It's only a cheap tin pencil and I never paid much attention to it."

Bullock put the pencil back in his pocket. "Funny thing you should have the same name as the man that was killed here," he observed. "Any relation?"

"My uncle."

"Uncle!" nearly shouted Bullock. "Are you Howard Torrent?"

The young man nodded. The Inspector had not yet recovered from his astonishment.

"What's a rich young fellow like you doing with a job like this?" he finally demanded.

"No law against taking a job, is there?"

"No," admitted the Inspector, "but I think all the same you'll have to take a little stroll with me up to police headquarters. Your being on the Exchange when your uncle was killed is just a little too pat to suit me."

"This is damn nonsense," protested Torrent. "Do you mean to say you're going to arrest me just because I happened to be near my uncle when he died?"

He pounded a clenched fist on the palm of his hand. "If you'd ever heard anything about the rules of the Stock Exchange you would know that clerks are not permitted to leave their posts during trading hours. Even if I'd wanted to kill my uncle, I couldn't have gone out on the trading floor."

Bullock looked inquiringly at Barton, and asked, "Is that so?" The other nodded in reply, "That's true."

The Inspector glowered angrily, and fiercely stroked his bristling mustache.

"All that may be so, and then again it mayn't," he declared. "But the fact remains that Philip Torrent was murdered, and we suspect that the owner of this red pencil is the guilty man. You've admitted it belonged to you, and so, under the circumstances, I'll have to bring you before the Police Commissioner. Come along, now—get your hat and we'll take a little ride uptown."

III

"FOR YOUR OWN SAKE, Torrent," pointed out -the Police Commissioner, "you'd better try to remember more about that pencil. You claim you lent it to someone who neglected to return it to you. We have reason to believe that pencil played a major part in the death not only of your uncle Philip Torrent, but of young Sandy Harrison as well."

"I don't care if it killed a thousand people, I still can't remember who borrowed it. After all, it was only a cheap tin affair— Why should I worry whether it was returned or not? Do you policemen keep track of every pencil in your pockets?" demanded Torrent passionately. "Is it a prison offence to swipe a pencil?"

Mackay raised his hand in a cautious gesture. "Now don't fly off the handle, young man. It's never done anyone any good in my experience—and that covers quite a few years. So just stay nice and quiet for a minute and I'll tell you a couple of things. If you're guilty it won't be news to you, and if you're innocent you might be able to help us to find your uncle's murderer."

He took a long puff at his cigar and settled back comfortably into his chair.

"First of all," he continued, "Philip Torrent and Sandy Harrison were poisoned by a South American poison named curare. This highly virulent poison must find its way into the blood stream via a cut or an injection. Now you, I am sure, think we are making mountains out of molehills about your red metal pencil that was found after the murders on the Stock Exchange floor. This is far from the case. I tell you in all seriousness that you should cultivate a most lively interest in the whereabouts of that pencil after it left your possession,

"And the reason is," he leaned over and tapped Torrent impressively on the arm, "the reason is, your life may depend on proving you lost the pencil. Less than an hour ago we discovered the point of that pencil was not a lead but a cleverly inserted phonograph needle."

The Commissioner paused. Both he and the Inspector were disappointed to see that Mackay's words had made no great impression on their prisoner.

"So what?" demanded Torrent. He looked at the two policemen with an appearance of genuine perplexity.

"That steel point was covered with a black substance which we have every reason to believe is poison," declared the Commissioner. "We further believe the murders were committed by a man who scratched the faces of his two victims with this cleverly improvised weapon."

Torrent stared at his two questioners with dismay. Gone was his arrogant air; he was now a badly scared young man.

Finally he collected his wits enough to make a reply.

"I don't know anything about either the death of my uncle or of Mr. Harrison except what I read in the newspapers, and you can't pin anything on me.

"We can try," Bullock reminded him grimly. "Don't think you're the only suspected person who claimed he was innocent."

The Commissioner drew another long puff on his cigar and blew smoke rings in wide circles above his head. He meditated for a moment. "Do you know, Mr. Torrent, that you're a person who had both motive and opportunity to kill your uncle? I think the District Attorney could build up quite a pretty little case against you, if you ask me. Dissolute young man—must have more money—hates his uncle—makes numerous threats—uncle finally is poisoned in nephew's presence. That's just the groundwork. The rest would be simple as pie to a good lawyer. I wouldn't give a nickel for your chances in front of a jury."

Torrent sat quietly in his chair. As far as he was concerned it looked as though he had said his last word.

"And then there's this—" pointed out Bullock. "We don't believe that—"

A sharp knock on the door made the Commissioner abruptly turn his head.

A police sergeant was standing on the threshold.

"Mr. Commissioner."

Mackay glanced impatiently at him. "Yes, Dolan, what is it?"

"I have a letter here," said Dolan. He unbuttoned his tunic and reached into an inside pocket.

A moment later the Commissioner had torn open the envelope and was scanning the contents of the short note.

The Inspector leaned over the desk as his superior finished reading the letter.

Mackay motioned to the sergeant who still was standing at attention near the Commissioner's desk.

"Take Mr. Torrent outside to the anteroom," he directed. "I'll let you know when I want him again."

Mackay waited with unconcealed impatience until Howard Torrent had been led from the room.

"This is a fine how-d'ye-do," he stated succinctly.

"Yeah?" demanded Bullock. "And how so?"

The Commissioner put one elbow on the broad expanse of his polished mahogany desk and pointed an abrupt finger at the Inspector.

"This note is from the Medical Examiner."

"O.K.," said Bullock, "and what did the old sawbones have to say?"

"Plenty!"

"He usually does," replied Bullock without interest. "I've always said he's a gassy old so and so."

"Well, I'll tell you what he told me. He's analyzed the black material on the phonograph needle—"

"Fine!"

"And he's just made his report."

"The poison, eh?"

"Unfortunately not," declared Mackay. "That black stuff—that virulent poison on the needle—that deadly curare—is what?"

"Don't ask me riddles," pleaded Bullock. "The only things I never could detect were cross-word puzzles. I'm still not sure whether an Emu is an African fish or a Chinese bird."

The Commissioner paid no attention to the Inspector's frivolity.

"There's only one thing wrong with our theory," he mourned, "and that is—it's all wrong."

"Yeah?" demanded Bullock, "and how so?"

"The Medical Examiner says in his own polite little way, 'What the devil are you bothering a busy man with your so-called poisoned phonograph needles for?'"

"So-called," ejaculated Bullock.

"Those are his words," said Mackay, "and I don't mind telling you he'll give me the burn-up number in a big way the next time he sees me. He writes that the needle point couldn't have been very dangerous. In fact, he said the black material consisted of lampblack—"

"Lampblack?" repeated Bullock, "what d'ye mean?"

"Soot to you," said the Commissioner wearily. "Let's hope it comes out in the wash."

9
HASTINGS DOES SOME EXPLAINING

BULLOCK LEFT the Commissioner's office with what might easily be called a severe case of the dumps. Not only had his pet theory concerning the poisoned pencil been proved unfounded, but he also had a feeling that the results of the analysis of the bottle of Brazilian Burnish might be equally disappointing. True enough, the poison, according to the doctors, had entered Sandy Harrison's body through the nail scratches; and yet it was an undisputed fact that these same scratches had been inflicted many hours before his murder. In addition, Bullock had been told that the results of the curare poisoning were apparent in a very short space of time. There couldn't be a connection between the nail polish and the murders; and yet it was a strange coincidence that Pedro, the South American hairdresser, had named his two nail polishes Brazilian Burnish and Paraguayan Polish. To Bullock's mind this implied that the man came originally from one of these adjoining countries, and in these two countries grew the noxious weed from which curare was derived.

The Inspector shook his head and upbraided himself roundly. "You're getting worse than Philo Vance," he said severely. "Pretty soon you'll be delivering a monologue on the marriage customs of the Paraguayan Indians."

Still figuratively shaking an admonishing finger in his own direction, the Inspector walked out of Police Headquarters, turned up Lafayette Street and presently entered his favorite rendezvous, a reformed speak-easy. He settled himself comfortably in a cozy corner and ordered an old-fashioned cocktail. A little early in the morning for this sort of thing, he reflected, but he soothed his conscience with the thought that, under the drink's mellow, stimulating glow, he might be able to evolve something to take the place of the recently shattered theory of the poisoned pencil.

He stared deep into his glass. Now, let's see: There were three men on the Exchange who might have killed Philip Torrent. There was Howard Torrent, his nephew, Temple Hastings, his partner, and Jack McDonald, his wife's lover. Each of these three had ample reason to murder. Howard Torrent for money, Temple Hastings for safety, Jack McDonald for love. If there were three more potent inducements, Bullock had never heard of them. Young Torrent, due to the fiasco of the metal pencil, would have to be eliminated from the investigation, at least temporarily. For the present, the Inspector decided to concentrate on McDonald and Hastings. Another visit to the Stock Exchange was plainly indicated.

He downed the remainder of his drink, paid his bill and a few moments later was bouncing downtown in an ancient taxi.

Logan, his friend the ex-policeman, was once more on duty in the lobby of n Wall Street. "Tell Mr. Jack McDonald I'd like to speak to him," he told the guard.

McDonald came out of the Exchange, recognized the Inspector and looked around uneasily as though he were apprehensive lest others be acquainted with Bullock's formidable face and form.

"Inspector," he said, "don't you think it would be more convenient if we went to the Luncheon Club to talk?"

Bullock made no objections; McDonald led the way upstairs. Due to the early hour the club was deserted. The two men walked into the lounge and took seats in a secluded spot.

"How about a glass of beer?" proposed the broker.

Bullock had none of the reserve so sedulously shown by detective-story detectives in refusing to drink with men they might be called upon to arrest.

"Sure," he answered promptly.

The Inspector removed the foam from his excellent bock beer in the orthodox manner. He took a deep draught, smacked his lips lustily, and inquired, "You were quite a friend of Philip Torrent?"

"Yes. We'd been friends for many years."

"How about Mrs. Torrent?" demanded Bullock bluntly.

"What do you mean?"

"I mean how friendly were you with her?" McDonald rose up angrily in his chair, but the look in Bullock's eyes brought him quickly to his senses.

"I was very fond of Mrs. Torrent," he finally admitted.

"Fond?"

"Yes—fond."

"Not in love, by any chance?" demanded Bullock.

The broker considered the question. He polished off his stein of beer, set it down empty on the table and turned to the Inspector. "Yes," he said, "I was, and I am, very much in love with Mrs. Philip Torrent."

"And what," asked Bullock, "did Mr. Torrent think of all that?"

"I asked him to give his wife a divorce so that she could marry me."

"And what was his answer?"

"He refused most emphatically," replied McDonald. "Not only emphatically but also insultingly!"

Bullock stroked his mustache judiciously. "Can't say as I blame him," he decided at last. "'Course, I'm not up on what Dorothy Dix says you should do in a case like that, but if anyone came to me and told me to get a divorce from my Maggie I'd sock him from here to California!"

Bullock took a long swig of his beer to assuage his righteous rage. He banged his stein down and demanded, "When did you last see Philip Torrent?"

"At lunch, the day he died."

"Do you mean you lunched with him?" inquired Bullock.

"I did."

"And what was your conversation—?"

"I asked him to divorce his wife."

"And he—?"

"He absolutely refused. In fact he became quite violent."

"Well, what would you expect?" asked the Inspector. "Did you think he'd fall on your neck and kiss you?"

"No, of course not," said McDonald. "However, since he'd been notoriously untrue to his wife over a period of many years, we thought that perhaps he might agree to a divorce."

"Had you broached this question before?"

"Yes, I had. And Mrs. Torrent also."

Bullock remained silent for a moment. Head bent, he sipped his beer reflectively; finally he looked up at the broker.

"Now, Mr. McDonald, was there anything unusual about your movements yesterday—that unfortunate day when your friend, Mr. Torrent, was murdered?"

"No. It was like every other day. I did my usual work. Executed the orders that were given to me to execute. Roamed all around the Stock Exchange as one usually does."

"Did you do any business in Air-Conditioning?"

"Why, surely. I had many trades in that stock."

"Do you remember the last time you were at Post 7, the Air-Conditioning crowd?"

"About a quarter past two, as I recall."

"You weren't there after that?"

"No."

"You weren't there when your friend Philip Torrent dropped dead?"

"What do you mean?" demanded McDonald furiously.

"I mean were you at Post 7 when your friend Philip Torrent dropped dead, that's what I mean."

McDonald's face grew crimson with rage. He opened his mouth, sputtered and closed it again.

"Certainly not," he finally managed to answer.

Bullock had tactfully ignored the broker's indignation. There was a certain hunting print on the wall that had suddenly become of great interest to the detective. The Inspector got up from his chair, examined the picture closely and sat down again.

"Where were you standing when the closing bell rang?" he asked.

McDonald knitted his brow; Bullock sat patiently waiting.

"I was executing an order in General Electric," the broker replied at last.

"So you were nowhere near Philip Torrent when he dropped dead?"

"For the second time, no. I might also add I didn't see Torrent on the Floor at any time during the day."

Bullock drained his stein. "Thanks," he said, "that's all I want to ask you."

McDonald escorted his visitor to the elevator; in the lobby he bade farewell, a little stiffly, to the Inspector.

Bullock walked toward Broadway with a stern frown on his face. "I didn't find out much, but I do know this—that fellow's a damn liar."

II

At the offices of *Torrent & Hastings* the surviving member of the firm sat in his private room in a distinctly cheerful frame of mind. That annoying Inspector of Police had not made a reappearance and for this Temple Hastings was extremely grateful. Probably the fright he had received yesterday was entirely uncalled for; but it certainly was lucky he had gone through his partner's desk before the police arrived. There had been several very important papers he was thankful the police hadn't discovered. On the whole, he decided, he had done a good job. He had left just the right amount of personal effects—just enough to discourage the suspicion that any of Philip Torrent's belongings had been removed.

Hastings leaned back in his chair completely satisfied.

A clerk entered. "Inspector Bullock calling, sir." With great difficulty Hastings kept his face from showing the consternation he felt. He put his finger into the neckband of his collar, waggled his head around, coughed, blew his nose and finally said, "Show him in."

"Good morning, Mr. Hastings," greeted Bullock on entering the room. "Here I am back again for a few more questions."

He reached into a pocket and produced two cigars. "Smoke?" he inquired of Hastings. The broker looked suspiciously at the gaudy green band and declined the offer.

Bullock put one of the cigars back in his pocket; with great deliberation he clipped the end of the other and lit up.

"Mr. Hastings," he finally asked, "what's all this I hear about your stealing a wad of your partner's money?"

Temple Hastings jerked back into his chair. "What!" he exclaimed. "What do you mean?"

"You heard me," declared Bullock, "and you don't need a dictionary to understand me."

"Who told you such a falsehood?" demanded the broker whose face, either from rage or fear, had suddenly become almost purple.

"Mrs. Torrent, for one," lied the Inspector blandly. "Seems she's been suspicious of you for some time."

"She'll regret that accusation," blustered Hastings.

"Maybe," Bullock replied calmly, "but in the meanwhile I suppose you won't object if I talk to your auditor."

"I most certainly do. It's an outrage the way you're handling this affair."

Bullock leaned forward until his face was scarcely a foot distant from the other's. "I know a more outrageous outrage," he said quietly. "D'ye know what that is?" He leaned even closer—"It's murder."

"Well," asked the broker, "what's that got to do with me?"

Bullock took another puff from his cigar. "Mr. Hastings, you told me yesterday you went straight from the Luncheon Club to your office. That was a lie. I've found out you were on the Stock Exchange at about two-forty."

Hastings shifted uncomfortably in his seat. There was something very disturbing in Bullock's cold, calculating gaze.

"That's correct," the broker admitted.

"Why did you lie to me?"

"I was afraid you might think I had something to do with Philip Torrent's death."

"I don't get that," protested Bullock. "I'm sure I gave you no reason to think I suspected you at all. However, that doesn't answer the question that's bothering me: Why did you go on the Exchange yesterday afternoon? I understand that although you've been a member for many years you seldom go on the Floor."

"That is also true," answered Hastings. "Philip executed the orders while I looked after the office work."

"When was the last occasion, previous to yesterday, that you went on the Stock Exchange?"

The broker had a worried look on his face as he replied: "It must have been at least six months ago."

"Rather an unfortunate coincidence that. I mean your picking yesterday of all days to change an established custom."

Hastings remained silent.

"But you still haven't told me your reason for going on the Stock Exchange yesterday," continued the Inspector.

Hastings stared out of a near-by window. Before he replied, he seemed to be carefully weighing the evils of two answers. Finally he sighed deeply and looked up at the detective.

"I'll tell you the whole story," he said, "even though I'm afraid it will put me in a decidedly precarious position."

He paused as though at a loss where and how to begin; at last he spoke.

"Yesterday morning, my partner, Philip Torrent, accused me of dishonesty. This I contended then, and still contend, was not the truth. Our firm has had losses—severe losses—in the conduct of our business—just as all brokers occasionally experience—but I was not personally responsible for these losses in any way, shape or form.

"My partner, however, gave notice he intended to dissolve our partnership and he threatened to prefer charges against me before the Governing Committee of the Exchange. If these charges had been pressed I was afraid that, even though I am innocent of any wrongdoing, I might be found guilty on a technicality and expelled from the Exchange.

"I have been a member of the Exchange for a great many years and I felt very keenly the possibility of this disgrace. All yesterday morning I brooded over my plight, and by lunch time, my nerves, which lately have been in a poor condition, completely went to pieces.

"Before lunch I had too many cocktails, during lunch I indulged in far too much wine, and after lunch I was not satisfied with one liqueur but ordered three. Consequently when the elevator deposited me at the Stock Exchange lobby I was in no condition to think clearly. All I remember is that my head rang with a chanting refrain—'You'll be expelled, you'll be expelled, you'll be expelled!'" Hastings paused and laid his hand on Bullock's shoulder. "And this," he pointed out, "is the part of my story I want you to believe."

The Inspector waited attentively.

"The reason I went on the Stock Exchange floor after luncheon yesterday was for the sake of sentiment."

"Sentiment!" echoed Bullock with surprise. "I don't follow you."

The broker tried to explain. "I had a fixed idea in my mind—due to my nerves and my drunken state—that I would be expelled from the Stock Exchange. Dominated by this thought I went on the Floor to have a last look around!"

Bullock drew a deep breath. "That's the damnedest explanation I've ever heard," he exclaimed. "But I'm not saying I don't believe you. It sounds just goofy enough to be true."

For a good two minutes the Inspector puffed away at the stub of his cigar and ruminated on the story he had just been told. Finally he came once more into action.

"Mr. Hastings," he inquired, "while you were on the Exchange yesterday did you see your partner, Philip Torrent?"

"No, I did not. But if I had I would have given him a wide berth. I had no wish to continue our altercation in a public place."

"D'ye know," observed the Inspector, "it's a funny thing. You claim you didn't see Philip Torrent, and Jack McDonald, who was on the floor of the Stock Exchange the whole session, says he didn't see him either. Now that seems strange, doesn't it?"

"In my case, no," was the reply. "To be frank, I was in such a condition I probably wouldn't have recognized anyone. I'm surprised, however, that an active broker like McDonald didn't run across my partner during the course of a full day's business."

"You said it," agreed Bullock. "It sounded just as peculiar to me. And there's another thing that strikes me as even odder. I told Barton, one of the Exchange's assistant secretaries, to find out for me, as tactfully as possible, what brokers were in the Air-Conditioning crowd at three o'clock—just before Torrent was stricken. He tells me he's having great difficulty in obtaining their names. I suppose they're all afraid of getting mixed up in a murder case."

"Quite possibly," assented Hastings, "and I don't blame them."

Bullock, lost in thought, did not hear this heretical remark. "If I only knew who was at that post!" he lamented. "With over a thousand brokers and God knows how many page boys and order clerks milling around, these murders have turned out to be the two toughest cases I've run up against in my twenty-three years on the Force."

Dolefully he shook his head from side to side while Hastings looked on suspiciously. The broker had cause to believe that Bullock's dour face was a permanent fixture, and was not due to the temporary setback which was at present disturbing his official peace of mind.

"I think I can tell you a way to find out the names of at least some of the brokers who were at Post 7 at the close yesterday," pointed out Hastings. "Not everyone who was there, mind you, but at least a few."

Bullock came back to earth with a pleasant thud. "How?" he demanded eagerly.

"I don't know whether you are aware of it or not, but my partner, Philip Torrent, was executing a very large buying order in International Air-Conditioning as the closing bell of the Exchange was sounded."

"Well," said Bullock, "what of it?"

Hastings answered, "When one buys there must be a seller, and if there's a seller one naturally takes down his name."

Bullock slapped his thigh vigorously and enthusiastically. "Mr. Hastings," he declared, "that bright idea of yours raises you just one thousand per cent in my estimation. Please get me the names of those sellers in a great big hurry."

Hastings pressed an electric push-button and one of his clerks appeared.

"Bring me Mr. Torrent's original report on the five thousand shares of Air-Conditioning he bought yesterday, just before he was murdered."

"Why didn't I see that report before this?" complained Bullock, after the boy had departed on his errand.

"I don't know," answered Hastings, "but I suppose Philip had given his trading reports to our floor clerks before the poison took effect. I understand it was several minutes after the close when the results of the poison became apparent."

The two men waited impatiently for the clerk's return. Finally he arrived and handed Hastings a blue slip of paper.

BUY

5000 TAC

Bought

700 — Logan & Kent @ 40 (64)

1100 — De Coppet & K @ 40

400 — Hewitt, G + A — 40

800 — P. G. & L — 40 (548)

400 — La Branche — 40

500 — Bondy H. — 40

100 — Straus, C — 40

1000 — Jack McDonald — 40½ (143)

5000

TORRENT AND HASTINGS

EAST WALL 28—T

"Here's the report on that last five thousand shares, sir," he said.

Hastings looked down the long list of names, pursed his lips and whistled softly.

"What d'ye find?" asked Bullock.

Hastings answered the question with a question. "Didn't you tell me McDonald said he hadn't seen Torrent on the floor yesterday?"

"Yes."

"That's interesting," replied the broker, shoving the order slip across the desk until it rested under the Inspector's nose. "The last words Phillip Torrent wrote in this world were these—"

Bullock's eyes slowly followed Hastings' finger down to the final penciled name.

10
TROUBLES OF A SPEAK-EASY PROPRIETOR

THE COMMISSIONER and Inspector Bullock were sitting with their heads very close together.

"This is the truth of the matter," said Bullock. "We've got a handful of suspects in Torrent's case and not one in Harrison's. As far as I can discover, Jack McDonald and Temple Hastings were merely on nodding acquaintance with Harrison, young Howard Torrent didn't even know him, Mrs. Torrent claims she never heard of him, and Lucy Laverne, although she was with him when he was poisoned, had only met him the previous day. Each of these people had excellent cause to murder Philip Torrent but none of them seems to have had anything against Sandy Harrison."

The Inspector rubbed his chin ruefully. "And yet," he continued, "there must be a connection, and a good one, between the two murders. The same hand killed both these men; all that is necessary for us to do is to find that common denominator we were talking about yesterday."

"That's all," agreed Mackay glumly.

"Now," observed Bullock, "since so many people had it in for Torrent it seems desirable for us to concentrate on his murderer. When we find him we automatically find the person who killed Harrison."

"That's true," said the Commissioner, "but it isn't as easy as you make it out to be."

Bullock nodded. "Don't I know that," he stated. "This whole rumpus has got me buffaloed. And why? Well, first of all, it's a funny thing that so many people connected with these cases have gone out of their way to lie to me. Of course, they can't *all* be guilty, but there seems to be a regular conspiracy of falsehood rearing up around us. To begin with, there's Temple Hastings. *He* lied. He told me he went straight back to his office after his lunch on the day of the murders; instead, I found he was on the Exchange at about the time Philip Torrent was murdered. Then there's McDonald. *He* lied. He told me he hadn't seen Torrent at any time on the Exchange yesterday; instead, I discovered he sold Philip Torrent one thousand shares of stock not a minute before Torrent fell to the floor, poisoned. Third, Mrs. Torrent took great pains to inform me McDonald was her husband's friend. *She* lied. Instead, I found that McDonald was her lover. Fourth, Lucy Laverne, although she had a woman's reason for murder, convinced me that she had everything to lose and nothing to gain by Torrent's death. *She* lied. We found later that Philip Torrent had left her fifty thousand dollars in his will—a fact that she probably was well aware of.

"We come now to Howard Torrent, the man who, to my mind, had most to gain by his uncle's death. We both thought we were sitting pretty when we found his red metal pencil with a phonograph needle in place of the lead. Unfortunately, this clue turned out to be a dud."

"True enough," began the Commissioner, "but there's one thing I—"

The telephone interrupted him. "Yes, he's here," said Mackay, handing the telephone to Bullock.

"Who is it?" demanded the Inspector. "Oh, yes, Dr. Moss."

Bullock pressed the receiver so closely to his face that his superior could not hear the choice flow of foul language that fairly burned the wire.

"I know, I know," Bullock protested. "But we have to try—that's what we're here for."

The Medical Examiner seemed not to have heard. A rasping screech was still pouring out of the instrument.

"I won't," said Bullock. "No, and he won't either. Yes, I understand. All right, goodbye."

He set the telephone down and mopped his brow. "Whew," was his only explanation.

"What's the big idea?" demanded Mackay.

"That little bottle of finger-nail polish I sent over to Moss to be analyzed," explained Bullock.

"The results were—?"

"About the same as our poisoned pencil. In other words—nothing!"

The two men sat in moody silence.

"You know," said Mackay finally, "that was a funny thing for Mrs. Torrent to do—to call up and tell us about Lucy Laverne being left that money. It almost looks as if she were trying to throw suspicion on the girl."

"Yeah," replied Bullock. "I'd thought of that myself. Of course that fifty thousand *did* give Lucy a good reason to murder Torrent. Since he and the girl had split one would assume that he'd change that part of his will at the first opportunity."

"That's true," admitted the Commissioner, "but we mustn't overlook Mrs. Torrent herself as a suspect, and a darn good one. She was madly in love with McDonald and I don't have to point out to you that her husband's death was exceedingly timely for her."

The telephone on the Commissioner's desk buzzed loudly again. He picked up the receiver.

"Oh, yes, Mrs. Torrent," he replied. "Yes, yes. I got your message."

He listened attentively.

"No. We haven't done anything like that," he told her. "For, the first place, we have no proof." His statement only seemed to enrage Mary Torrent. Her voice rose shrilly, and Bullock, sitting beside Mackay, could now hear every word. "I demand that you arrest that Laverne woman immediately and charge her with the murder of my husband."

The Commissioner winked broadly over the telephone at Bullock. "How could she murder him, Mrs. Torrent?" he inquired patiently. "Was she on the Stock Exchange yesterday afternoon?"

"Of course not!" cried out Mrs. Torrent. "*Naturally* she couldn't go on the Exchange, but she had Sandy Harrison murder my husband and later she killed Harrison to cover up her tracks."

"Come! come! Mrs. Torrent!" expostulated Mackay. "That's a bit far-fetched."

"Perhaps it is, but it's the only plausible way to explain the two deaths."

"It's an ingenious theory," admitted the Commissioner, "but it's as full of holes as a sieve. As a matter of fact, Mrs. Torrent, we could make almost the same accusation against you—that you had your friend McDonald kill Philip Torrent so that you two could marry."

"That's perfectly ridiculous," stormed Mary Torrent.

The Commissioner held the telephone receiver far away from his ear, and waited for her angry tirade to subside.

"By the way," he finally inquired, "where were you yesterday afternoon at three o'clock?"

"At my lawyer's."

"Where is his office?"

"At One Wall Street."

"One Wall Street!" ejaculated Mackay. "That's next door to the Exchange!"

"Yes," agreed Mrs. Torrent. "And what of it?"

Mackay, ignoring the question, changed the subject abruptly. "Did you see your husband yesterday?" he demanded.

"Not alive," was the answer. "I was still asleep when he left to go downtown. In any event, I very seldom saw him before dinner—we occupied separate bedrooms."

"May I ask," inquired the Commissioner in his most suave tones, "what was the reason for the visit to your lawyer's?"

There was no hesitation in the reply. "I had been consulting my attorney as to the possibility of obtaining a divorce. Unfortunately, my husband once more refused point-blank to give me my freedom."

"You mean he was present with your lawyer?" asked Mackay.

"No. I spoke to him over the telephone. He was on the Exchange at the time."

"And what time was that?" the Commissioner inquired.

"About a quarter to three."

Mackay put his hand over the transmitter of the telephone and demanded hoarsely, "Got anything you want to ask her, Bullock?"

The Inspector shook his head. "I've a couple of questions, but I'm going to ask them when we're face to face. I don't care for this long distance question and answer game. Too easy for her to lie and get away with it."

II

BULLOCK SWUNG OFF the Sixth Avenue Elevated at 50th Street, descended to the pavement and walked uptown. At 51st Street he turned east for several blocks. Presently he stopped before a brownstone house.

"So this is Chipo Marinelli's place," observed the Inspector to himself. "Not many joints like this any more. The hotel bars have run them all out of business."

He stepped up to the entrance way and pressed the bell. He waited for a minute, then a small shutter opened in the door and a pair of eyes peered out.

"Mr. Marinelli in?" Bullock inquired.

"Maybe," said the two eyes. "Who wants him?"

"Tell him Inspector Bullock of Headquarters would like to impose on his valuable time—just a few minutes, you understand."

The peephole closed with a snap and Bullock heard retreating footsteps. Presently there were voices in the areaway, the door was thrown open and a swarthy, rather good-looking young Italian stood facing him.

"Chipo Marinelli?" asked Bullock.

"Yes, Inspector."

"I've got a few questions, Marinelli; nothing to do with your business here," he added reassuringly.

The Italian looked relieved. He held the door open wide. Bullock followed him into the bar which occupied the front of the house.

It was a gaily decorated little drinking place, and, before the blight that had descended so miraculously on speak-easy proprietors, had evidently done a considerable amount of business. At the present moment there were but two customers, who sat forlornly in a corner, listlessly chatting with the bartender.

"It's quiet enough here, Inspector," said Marinelli, "but I guess we'd better be all alone, heh?"

Without waiting for an answer he pushed open a swinging door and led the way into the adjoining dining-room. He pointed out a table and the two men sat down.

"Have a drink?" Marinelli inquired of the Inspector.

"Sure. Make it beer."

A minute or two later the barman deposited two large foaming glasses on the table.

"Marinelli," said Bullock after he had taken a deep draught of his beer, "I understand you had a little trouble yesterday?"

The Italian nodded sourly. "Some guy down at the S.L.A. has it in for me. They won't give me any peace."

"How often have you tried to get a liquor license?" demanded the Inspector.

"About fifty times," answered Marinelli, "but it's no go."

Bullock raised his eyebrows significantly. "What seems to be the trouble?"

"We had a shooting here last year," replied the proprietor frankly. "You guys tried to pin it on me. They say I'm a bad character, or what have you, and I ain't fit to be in the lily white liquor business."

Marinelli's lips twisted into a sneer. "Anyhow, that's their story. The real slant is there's too many places selling booze on this street. Somebody had to be the goat and I got elected."

Bullock clucked his tongue in sympathy. "That sure is tough, Marinelli, but what I came to see you about was this—" He paused, and looked Marinelli in the eye. "Why did you telephone Philip Torrent yesterday afternoon?"

The Italian stared back at the detective without a trace of perturbation in his face.

"Why'd I call Mr. Torrent? Who told you I called him?"

"Can the dumb chatter," directed Bullock. "We know you phoned him. You can save yourself a lot of time and trouble by telling me right now what you wanted of him."

Marinelli pushed his chair back against the wall, put his fingers in the armpits of his checkered waistcoat and crossed his legs leisurely. "And just why should I do that?" he inquired serenely.

"You don't *have* to tell me, Mr. Marinelli," pointed out Bullock with exaggerated affability. "But I think it might be very, very advisable if you did."

The speak-easy proprietor considered all the aspects of this scarcely concealed threat. "Oh, well," he finally answered, "there's no reason not to. He was a damn good customer in the old days and when I got in a jam yesterday I called him up because I thought he might bail me out."

"And did he?"

"No. He told me to go chase myself."

"Who finally put up the jack?"

"My mouthpiece."

"How much?" demanded the Inspector.

"A hundred bucks."

Bullock pursed his lips and made an excessively rasping noise. "That's a lot of monkey dust, and you know it!"

"Oh, yeah?" said Marinelli.

"You know and I know," declared Bullock, "you didn't have to call anybody in this world to put up a lousy hundred dollar bail."

Marinelli shrugged his shoulders. "Well, that's my story and it's the truth."

"I suppose you read the papers," suggested the Inspector.

"Sure."

"You read that your friend Torrent got bumped off?"

"Oh, sure."

"Didn't mean much to you, eh?"

"I won't say that, Inspector—you know, old customer and all."

Bullock raised his glass of beer; he had been so busy asking questions he had almost forgotten its existence. He downed the dregs with a gulp and stood up to leave. "So you can't tell me anything about Mr. Torrent's murder?"

"Not me!" declared Marinelli. "I said he was an old customer—one of the bunch that used to think I had a swell joint, but I haven't seen him in months."

The Inspector picked up his hat from a near-by table, and said, "O.K. I'll be going now."

Marinelli opened the dining-room door and escorted his unwelcomed caller to the front door.

He shook hands with Bullock and a moment later the Inspector found himself standing on the curb, signaling a taxi.

He stepped into the cab, told the man to drop him off at Centre Street, and settled back against the leather cushions.

His driver started off with the usual jerk; Bullock closed his eyes in anticipation of the long drive downtown.

The cab had barely gone ten feet when the brakes were suddenly slammed on and Bullock was thrown violently onto the floor.

With a series of curses, the Inspector regained his seat, and stared over his driver's shoulder at a taxi, which, disregarding all traffic rules, had cut into the curb in front of them.

His hand reached out for the doorknob; this reckless driver would not escape without a summons. He was halfway out of his cab when a girl jumped from the offending car, gave the driver a handful of change and crossed the sidewalk to Chipo Marinelli's.

Bullock caught only a glimpse of her face but that was sufficient. It was Lucy Laverne.

11
ALARMS AND EXCURSIONS

BULLOCK STARTED to follow Lucy Laverne back into the speak-easy, but when he was halfway across the sidewalk an arresting thought struck him: After all she had every right to go into Marinelli's and he had no plausible excuse to follow her in.

He shook his head with perplexity. What to do? Return to the speak-easy and ask the girl the reason for her visit? No. That would be a foolish move. She would probably reply that she had come for the very natural purpose of getting a drink. Should he wait until she had left the restaurant and then return to question Marinelli as to her visit?

Certainly, in any event it was most peculiar that Lucy Laverne would go to a speak-easy rather than to a smart hotel bar for an afternoon cocktail. The only obvious answer to this anomaly was that she had visited Marinelli's for some other purpose—and that purpose, Bullock was certain, could only be connected with either Harrison's or Torrent's death. Finally, torn between a desire for action and a feeling of caution, Bullock decided that discretion was indeed the better part of valor. He climbed back into his cab and started downtown. On his way south he turned over in his mind the events of the afternoon.

In as far as Lucy Laverne was concerned, there was no occasion to worry lest she give them the slip. Mulligan, assuredly, had her under the very closest surveillance. Later in the day, Bullock would receive a full report of her goings and comings.

Presently, the taxi stopped at police headquarters and the Inspector hurried upstairs to the Commissioner's offices. Mackay sat in silence while Bullock told of his trip to Marinelli's, the Italian's explanation of the telephone call to Torrent and Lucy Laverne's visit to the speak-easy.

"That fellow's a smooth article," observed the Commissioner when the Inspector had finished his story. "I've got a hunch he's more mixed up in these murders than we think. He evidently knows Lucy Laverne, he admits he was friendly with Torrent, and it wouldn't surprise me very much if a play-boy like Sandy Harrison had also patronized his speak-easy."

Bullock nodded in agreement. "Chipo Marinelli's nobody's fool," he declared. "He knows what it's all about. He's been around—plenty."

Mackay didn't seem to be listening. He banged his fist down on his desk with a resounding thump. "My God," he sputtered, "What a couple of saps we've been!"

The Inspector raised his eyebrows questioningly. "How so?" he demanded.

"C. M.," shouted the Commissioner, "Chipo Marinelli!"

"Holy Cats," ejaculated Bullock. "You mean the seventy thousand dollar item in Torrent's papers that no one seems to know anything about?"

"I do."

Bullock looked at his superior with admiration. "Chief, I think you've hit it smack on the head; but how in the world could Marinelli owe Torrent all that money?"

"Maybe Torrent lent it to him to open up a speak-easy," suggested the Commissioner. "You'd be surprised how many so-called respectable people used to own pieces of our best speaks. It wasn't all gangster money that kept those places running—not by a long shot."

"That's as good an idea as any," agreed the Inspector, rising to his feet. "Well, no rest for the weary. I'll go back and see Marinelli again."

Soon the Inspector was knocking once more at Marinelli's shuttered entrance. This time the doorman, recognizing him, opened the door promptly. 'Where's Marinelli?" said Bullock.

"Sorry, Inspector," answered the man, "he ain't here now—gone out for a while. He'll be back later."

"I'll wait," declared the Inspector. He hung his hat and coat on a hook in the corridor, walked into the bar and perched himself on a high stool.

"Make mine an old-fashioned," he directed the bartender.

"Right away, Inspector," replied the man who evidently had been informed of Bullock's identity.

The Inspector took an approving sip of his cocktail and addressed the barman, "Not much business, eh?"

The bartender shrugged his shoulders expressively. "What can you expect? We're just hanging on by an eyebrow. Nobody wants to come to a little dump like this any more when they can go to a swell hotel café."

He picked up a glass and began industriously to polish it. "The wonder is that Chipo's kept going as long as this. Of course," he continued, "if he had to pay rent he'd have folded up long ago."

"How d'ye mean?" demanded Bullock. "Does he own this building?"

"Sure, it's his—no mortgage either."

Bullock whistled softly. "Then he doesn't have to worry! Buildings on this street, even in these days, are nice little things to own."

The barman grunted in reply and went on with his polishing. Bullock finished his drink and ordered another.

"When did he buy this house?" the Inspector inquired when he had helped himself to his whisky.

"About four years ago."

"He must have more sense than most of his friends," commented Bullock. "A lot of speak-easy proprietors nowadays have nothing left except a swell collection of rubber checks."

He took a long swig of his drink. "Hasn't Marinelli any vices?" he asked after he had wiped his mouth with the back of his huge hand.

"None, except the stock market."

"What—still?" demanded Bullock incredulously.

"Sure," replied the bartender. "He was one of the wise guys—went short the market in nineteen-thirty and cleaned up. He had some sort of a relative down in Wall Street that gave him tips."

"Humph," remarked Bullock sourly. "We all had one of those."

Just then the door to the dining-room opened and a woman entered.

"Good evening, Joe," she said.

"Evening, Mrs. Marinelli."

She walked over to the bar and settled herself comfortably on a stool.

"Give me a bacardi," she directed the bartender. Soon the foamy white mixture was placed before her; she took a sampling sip and turned Bullock. "You're waiting for my husband?"

"Yes. Will he be back soon?"

"I think so," she answered. "He went out right after you left this afternoon; he said he'd be home around six."

Bullock sat chatting with the woman for half an hour; six o'clock came and there was still no sign of Marinelli.

Maria Marinelli was finishing her second bacardi and the Inspector his third old-fashioned, when there was a clatter of feet in the adjoining dining-room, the door burst open and two small children came tumbling into the bar.

The woman jumped down quickly from her stool and waved a stern finger in their direction. "Go upstairs," she commanded. "You're a couple of bad, bad children."

The children took to their heels; Maria Marinelli returned to the bar, picked up her drink, drained the remainder and said good-night to Bullock.

After her departure Bullock lit a cigar and leaned back with that fine glow of contentment which can only be produced by a judicious mixture of tobacco and whisky.

"Good looking girl, that," he observed to the bartender.

"You said it," replied Joe. "And the boss sure is nuts over her."

"Nice looking kids, too," continued Bullock.

"They're twins," explained the barman, "and she's got six-year-old triplets too!"

"You don't say," said Bullock. "That's kinda unusual—what are they—boys?"

"A mixture," replied Joe. "The twins are boys and the triplets are two girls and a boy."

Bullock, bubbling over with good fellowship, became very paternal. "I've got two myself," he said. "Great thing to have kids around the house."

The bartender was sceptical. "They can be an awful nuisance," he pointed out. "Mrs. Marinelli's triplets raise holy hell around here, but she's so crazy about them that they never get the wolloping they need."

The Inspector wagged his head up and down solemnly.

"And she's given them the damnedest names," went on Joe. "She named them Cataldino, Mazeta, and Lorenzana—how's that for a couple of mouthfuls?"

Bullock laughed and threw up his hands in mock horror.

"Where'd she find those monikers?"

"She's one of these religious bugs," said Joe. "She told me they were named after three priests."

"They're pretty flossy names," admitted Bullock, "but I'm a bit inflicted in that direction myself—my middle name is Xavier."

A telephone in the corner of the room started to ring; Joe stepped from behind the bar and entered the booth.

"Hello," he said. "Sure, Boss. It's me."

He received some orders from Marinelli.

"O.K., Boss, I'll—"

"Tell him I'm here," interrupted Bullock, "and I want to see him."

Joe followed these instructions and then shouted across the room.

"He's over in Jersey. Says he'll see you in the morning."

Bullock gave vent to a series of curses. "Tell him I'll be here at ten o'clock tomorrow."

The bartender relayed the message and returned to the bar.

"Well," said the Inspector, "I might as well be drunk as the way I am. Give me another old-fashioned!"

II

"What's that, Mulligan?" demanded the Police Commissioner incredulously, "You lost her! Well, you're a fine specimen to be on the Force—can't even follow a girl without letting her slip away."

"I couldn't help it, Chief. She went to a beauty parlor in a building on the corner of 58th Street and Madison Avenue and I waited outside for three hours. Finally the place closed for the day and all the people that work there went away. I didn't want to ask any of them about Laverne, but I spoke to the elevator man in the building and he told me she'd gone out a different entrance."

"Why didn't you know there were two ways out?" inquired Mackay heatedly.

"Well, even if I had known I couldn't've been in two places at once," complained the unhappy Mulligan.

"You could have notified the cop on the beat, couldn't you? In five minutes he'd have got another man from the station house to help you."

"I'm sorry, Commissioner, but—"

"Nuts," said Mackay. He slammed down the telephone receiver on its hook and glared across the room at his secretary, who was standing on the threshold.

"Inspector Bullock's here, sir. Shall I show him in?"

Mackay grunted something unintelligible which the secretary seemed to have no trouble in interpreting.

Bullock walked into the office.

"Here's a fine one," commented the Commissioner, without preliminaries. "That fool Mulligan let Laverne slip away from him."

The Inspector whistled loudly. "By accident d'ye think or did she try to give him the goodbye?"

"I don't know," answered the Commissioner. Bullock leaned back in his chair and lit a cigarette. "Well, now we won't know where she went after she left Chipo Marinelli's."

He puffed away at the cigarette. "I don't suppose it'll make much difference—she's probably home by now. Mulligan can pick her up again."

"Um," said Mackay. "Anyhow it's slip-shod work." He changed the subject abruptly. "How about Marinelli?" he asked.

"He wasn't there when I got back; I'm going to see him in the morning."

The Commissioner began searching, through a mass of papers that littered the surface of his desk.

"Do you remember what the Medical Examiner said about curare?" he inquired. "How this poison was so hard to get and that practically no one, except doctors, had ever heard of it?"

"Yes," replied Bullock. "He told me the only time he'd ever seen any of it was when he was attending medical college. They use it for some kind of an experiment with frogs."

The Commissioner at last found the paper he was hunting for. He spread it out in front of him, and asked, "Do you also remember what Mrs. Torrent told us about young Howard Torrent—about what a no-good person he was, in all kinds of nasty scrapes, fired from college, breach of promise actions—?"

"Yes, I remember," said Bullock.

"I've been checking up on that young man," continued Mackay. "And here's the report I got an hour or so ago."

He handed the typewritten statement to the Inspector. "You'll note on the second page a very interesting item: the college he was fired from was the Harvard Medical School."

12
THERE ARE TWO KINDS OF POISON

NEXT MORNING, promptly at ten o'clock, Bullock arrived at Marinelli's. The Italian met him at the front door and escorted him into the dining-room.

"Marinelli," said the Inspector, driving straight to the point, "why did Lucy Laverne come here yesterday?"

"She's an old customer," he replied promptly; "she often drops in for a cocktail."

"Sure it wasn't for another reason?" persisted Bullock. "Sure it wasn't for the purpose of having a private little chat with you?"

"It was not," stated Marinelli emphatically. "She came for a drink—she still comes here regularly; she's about the only one of the old crowd that does."

Bullock leaned across the table, and demanded, "Are you sure she didn't call yesterday to talk to you about the seventy thousand dollars you owe Torrent?"

Marinelli jerked back in his chair, an expression of dismay creeping over his face. "What! Me owe Mr. Torrent seventy thousand dollars! That's a hot one!"

"You deny it?"

"I sure do. I never owed him a cent in my life!"

"Among Mr. Torrent's papers," observed Bullock, "there is a memo which indicates otherwise."

"I'd like to see that paper," said Marinelli. "I don't believe it says I owe him all that money."

"You can see it any time you want to drop down to Headquarters," replied Bullock.

"All right, I'll go down there now. We might as well get this thing settled."

"That suits me, Marinelli. Let's go."

A few minutes later the two men left the restaurant, and, hailing a taxi, started on their way downtown.

On arriving at Centre Street they went directly to the Commissioner's offices.

"This is Marinelli, Chief," said Bullock. "He wants to look at that memo we found in Torrent's desk."

Mackay opened a drawer and produced a small slip of paper. He presented it to Marinelli without comment.

The Italian looked at it for a moment and handed it back. "You don't call that evidence, do you? Just the initials C.M. and I'm supposed to owe him seventy grand."

"We don't call it conclusive evidence," replied Mackay, "but we think those initials mean you." He leaned back in his chair and crossed his legs. "By the way, where'd you get the money to buy that house of yours?"

"I made it."

"How?"

"In the liquor business."

The Police Commissioner picked up a folio of typewritten sheets. "According to our records you opened your speak-easy in January, 1931. Previous to that you were a waiter at the Hotel Manhattan. Now where did you get the money to start your place? From waiter to prominent speak-easy proprietor overnight is quite a jump."

Marinelli shrugged his shoulders. "You think you know the whole works, but you don't. As a matter of fact I made the money in the stock market."

"In nineteen-thirty?" demanded Mackay incredulously.

Marinelli nodded in reply.

"I suppose you can prove this?"

"Sure. The books of the firm where I traded will show."

"What's the name of that firm?"

"Mr. Torrent's—*Torrent & Hastings*."

"Oh, ho!" exclaimed Bullock, "so Torrent comes into the picture again?"

"What if he does? I've never denied that Mr. Torrent was a friend of mine. In the old days, he and Miss Laverne used to be at my place two or three times a week."

"Well," said Mackay, "let's leave Torrent out of the story for a few minutes. How about Harrison? You knew him, didn't you?"

"Sure. He used to drop in sometimes."

"A friend of Torrent's?"

"Not particularly. I suppose they knew each other on the Exchange, but I never saw them out on parties together."

"Did you ever see Harrison and Lucy Laverne together?"

"No."

"Do you know Mrs. Philip Torrent by sight?"

"No."

"Or Jack McDonald?"

"Never heard of him."

"Or Howard Torrent, Mr. Torrent's nephew?"

"No."

"Or Temple Hastings?"

"Certainly," replied Marinelli. "I had my stock account with *Torrent & Hastings*. I used to see a lot of Mr. Hastings. I saw him almost every day for several months."

Mackay looked inquiringly over at Bullock. "Anything more you want to ask him?"

The Inspector shook his head, and Mackay motioned toward the door.

"You can go now, Marinelli," said the Commissioner.

Marinelli got up and prepared to leave. "I don't suppose you could do anything about my liquor license?" he asked Mackay. "Those guys down at the State Liquor Authority say the reason they won't fix me up is because I've got a bad police record."

The Commissioner did not immediately reply; he appeared to be seriously considering the request.

"I don't see any reason why we should do anything," he finally told the man. "If you want *me* to help *you*, you'll have to help *us* in this Torrent-Hastings case. You're holding back something and I know it. When you tell us what that is, I might do something about your license."

II

THE COMMISSIONER picked up the telephone receiver. "Oh, it's you, Mulligan," he growled.

He listened attentively. "Didn't come home? Well, I'll be double damned!"

He spoke over his shoulder to Bullock who was standing near by. "Laverne skipped. She didn't come home last night and the maid says she hasn't heard from her."

The Commissioner turned back to the telephone. "Inspector Bullock will be up there in a few minutes; meanwhile you stay in her apartment and keep an eye on her maid."

Twenty minutes later Bullock strode into the too elaborately furnished lobby of the Alden Apartments and hastened upstairs.

The door was opened by the very much agitated maid; behind her Mulligan stood watchfully waiting.

"Any news?" the Inspector demanded.

"No, sir," replied Mulligan. "I guess she's flown the coop."

Bullock frowned, and turned abruptly to the colored girl.

"What do you know about all this?" he asked fiercely.

"'Deed I don' know nuthin', Mr. Inspector; 'deed I don'. Miss Lucy, she tole me she's goin' to have her curls primped and come straight home; and she jest ain't come home."

"Is Miss Laverne in the habit of staying out all night without calling you up?"

"No, suh. She sure ain't. Never did nuthin' like this befo'."

"What d'ye think happened to her?" inquired Bullock.

"She's daid," said the colored girl without a moment's hesitation. "—daid, just as sho' as yo' is sittin' there where yo' is."

"I don't think it's as bad as all that," chuckled Bullock. "I'm afraid you've been reading too many of Miss Laverne's mystery novels. She's got a grand collection of them, I know. I spent a couple of hours with a very gory one the last time I was here."

"She's daid, daid," repeated the girl, burying her face in her apron and bursting into a paroxysm of tears.

Bullock gave Mulligan a significant look and jerked his finger in the direction of the kitchen. The detective was quick to take the hint, and a moment later he led his weeping charge out of the room.

As soon as the kitchen door closed, Bullock entered the bedroom and opened the top drawer of the dressing table. He rummaged through the very personal belongings of the missing girl, and having found nothing of interest in the dressing table, proceeded to search the bureau.

He went through everything with meticulous care—through piles of lacy underwear, silken pajamas and other feminine frills, the very uses of which he was entirely ignorant. Presently, in the lowest drawer, hidden beneath a heap of stockings, he came upon a tissue-paper-wrapped package. Carefully he unrolled the paper from around a long hard object. As the last folds of tissue unwound, he gave a cry of astonishment. On the palm of his hand rested a glass and nickel hypodermic needle, half filled with an amber-colored liquid.

He stared with fascinated eyes at this totally unexpected find. Finally, he carefully remade the package, taking care not to touch the hypodermic for fear of obliterating possible fingerprints; then, walking over to the dressing table, he gingerly picked up a silver hand-mirror, and wrapped it in a towel, which he took from the adjoining bathroom.

He spent another ten minutes examining the contents of a desk that occupied a corner of the sitting room; but there he found nothing save an assortment of receipted bills, a few newspaper clippings and a bundle of cancelled bank checks.

At last, with a final glance around the diminutive entrance hall, he walked into the kitchen where Mulligan was keeping watch over the maid.

"Stick around here," the Inspector instructed the detective. "'Til call you from downtown in a couple of hours. Let me know immediately if Laverne phones or comes back."

III

"It's as plain as the nose on your face," said Mackay inelegantly. "Laverne told us that she had Torrent called out to the Stock Exchange lobby about twenty minutes before three; approximately twenty minutes later he dropped dead. She was with Sandy Harrison in his office at three minutes after three, and twenty minutes later he also was dead.

"Now since Dr. Moss told us it took about twenty minutes for curare to kill a man, it's perfectly obvious she stuck them both with that hypo."

"Maybe," replied Bullock doubtfully. "But there's a certain amount of pain attached to having a needle jabbed into you. If Laverne attacked Torrent, it's funny he didn't make some fuss about it."

The Commissioner dismissed the objection airily. "It doesn't hurt much. Besides, she said he was very upset and embarrassed about her calling to see him, and the last thing in the world he would want would be a scene in the Stock Exchange lobby."

"It's a good theory, Chief—all but for one point. Dr. Moss told us the poison entered Torrent's right ear. Surely she couldn't have jabbed his ear out in the middle of the Stock Exchange lobby? There's always fifty or more people milling around and somebody would certainly have seen her doing it."

"That hypodermic is a pretty small one," Mackay replied. "It could be almost concealed in her hand. Besides, Dr. Moss may be wrong in saying the poison entered through a cut on the ear."

"I don't think so," objected Bullock decisively. "There's the two handkerchiefs we found in the dead men's pockets. Both handkerchiefs were spotted with small blood stains which looked to me like the kind you put on towels after you've cut yourself shaving. Sometime between the hour they dressed and the hour they died, Torrent and Harrison used their handkerchiefs to wipe away a small amount of blood from their *faces*."

"Not necessarily," declared the Commissioner. "The blood might have come from cuts on their hands."

"Well, Chief," said Bullock, getting up out of his chair, "there's only one way to find out and that's to look. The bodies are still at the Morgue. I'll go around and see if there're any other cuts on their bodies. At the same time I'll be able to get a report from the Medical Examiner about the liquid we found in the hypo. If it's curare it's going to be just too bad for Lucy."

IV

BULLOCK DROVE uptown over cobble-stoned Avenue A, and presently arrived at that gloomy, sinister building which houses both the Medical Examiner's offices and the Morgue, where unfortunate victims of accident and crime rest forlornly on cold marble slabs.

Dr. Moss received him jovially and immediately offered him a drink. "And it's not embalming fluid, either," he added.

After toasting the Medical Examiner's health, Bullock got down to business.

"It's about those cuts on the bodies," he said. "The Old Man thinks that you might be wrong about the poison coming in *via* their faces."

"Baloney," replied Dr. Moss emphatically. "The scratch marks on the left side of Harrison's face and the cut on Torrent's right ear were the places the poison entered. There's not the slightest doubt. Both Dr. Martin, his assistant, and myself are as one on that point."

"O.K.," replied the Inspector. "Then that's that."

He took another long swallow of Dr. Moss's excellent bourbon.

"How about the liquid in the hypo. Have you found out what it is?"

"They're working on it down at the laboratories now," answered the Medical Examiner. "They should be finished by this time."

He rang a bell and a white-coated intern appeared in the doorway.

"Find out for me," Dr. Moss directed, "if the fluid in a hypodermic needle, which I sent downstairs an hour ago, has been analyzed."

The man soon returned holding in his hand a sheet of paper.

"Here's the report, sir."

The Medical Examiner glanced rapidly down the page, and, with a quizzical smile, presented the sheet to Bullock.

Bullock read the short typewritten statement, frowned deeply and handed it back to the doctor. “So it isn’t curare?”

“No,” said Dr. Moss. “It’s just plain insulin.”

“What’s that?” asked Bullock, “a poison?”

“In a fashion,” answered the Medical Examiner, “but you’d hardly be interested in it. It’s used in the treatment of diabetes and its mission is to save life, not to kill.”

13
WANTED: FIFTY THOUSAND DOLLARS

In the dignified law offices of Rosen, Hargrave, Randell and Smart there was an unusual stir. For the first time in the long and honored history of the firm there had arrived, what Mr. Hargrave, with much hemmings and hawings, had very correctly labeled, a "blackmailing communication."

This letter had been delivered with the midday mail, and, at a hurriedly called conference of all the members of the firm, it had been decided that Mr. Hargrave, as a close friend of the Police Commissioner's, should go to Headquarters and lay the matter before the proper authorities.

Therefore, when Bullock returned from his abortive visit to the Medical Examiner's offices, he found Mr. Hargrave deep in consultation with Mackay.

After being introduced to the distinguished visitor he was shown the typewritten letter that had caused so much commotion:

> "Dear Sirs"
> "Since you are executors of the estate of the late Philip Torrent, we demand that you carry out the following instructions.
>
> "By the will of Philip Torrent, Miss Lucy Laverne was left fifty thousand dollars. Get this money at once in twenty dollar bills—put them in a brown-paper package and address it to Harvey Jones, Box 817, P.O. Station O. Then at six o'clock tonight have

your messenger mail the package in the letter box at the corner of Sixth Avenue and Twenty-eighth Street. If you don't do this, Miss Laverne's blood will be on your hands.

Q—"

At the bottom of the page were these scribbled words: "Do as they ask, for God's sake—Lucy Laverne."

Bullock looked across the desk and Mackay significantly winked an eye.

"She's pretty smooth, eh?" observed the Commissioner.

"What!" exclaimed Mr. Hargrave in astonishment. "You think that girl wrote the whole letter herself?"

"Sure," replied Mackay, "of course she did."

Bullock shook his head vigorously. "I don't believe it. That letter's the real stuff. Somebody read in the papers about her being left fifty thousand dollars and thought it was a nice opportunity to collect it for themselves."

"Perhaps," said the Commissioner sceptically, "but it looks to me as though she knows too much about the murders and she wanted to make a getaway. To do this she needed money—and plenty of it—so she thought up this bright scheme to obtain Torrent's bequest without having to come out of hiding."

"I don't believe it," repeated the Inspector. "All this stuff about mailing the package in a certain mail box and addressing it to Harvey Jones,—it doesn't sound like a woman's idea."

The Commissioner waved his hand in a gesture of impatience. "That's the very reason I think she cooked up the whole thing. It's all so amateurish. No regular crook would ever try to pull anything that raw. What are we supposed to be doing when the mythical Mr. Harvey Jones appears at the post office to collect the ransom? I've been on the Police Force for thirty years and I've heard of five hundred different ways of delivering money to kidnappers—but sending fifty thousand dollars to a box in a United States post office is a brand new one for me. It's just too silly to be anything but the crazy idea of a frightened girl."

"All right," said Bullock, "then what're we going to do?"

He glanced inquiringly at Mr. Hargrave.

The lawyer toyed with his eyeglasses and looked exceedingly uncomfortable.

"I scarcely know what to say," he replied at last. "Legally the whole affair presents any number of difficulties. Although the estate has not, as yet, been probated, still we *could* pay out the money if it were absolutely necessary. I would, however, be loathe to take such an action unless I were quite satisfied in my own mind that the postscript of this ransom letter was unmistakably in Miss Laverne's handwriting."

Bullock picked up the letter, and studied the handwriting once more.

"I spent an hour or so at Miss Laverne's apartment this morning," he observed. "While there, I had occasion to go through her desk. I examined a great many specimens of her handwriting and I have no hesitation in saying she wrote this last sentence, 'Do as they ask, for God's sake—Lucy Laverne.'"

"That makes our position—I mean the position of my firm—even more unfortunate," pointed out Hargrave. "If we refuse to send this woman's abductors the money which is rightfully hers we put her in jeopardy of her life."

The lawyer pursed his lips, placed the fingertips of his two hands together and assumed a most judicial air. "As far as I can see," he went on, "it would, perhaps, be best to accede to her desire. If, as the Inspector has stated, this is her signature, we are amply protected at law."

"You don't need any law," said the Police Commissioner, "and you won't need to be protected either, for the simple reason that that money will never get to the kidnappers. We'll take that package when it reaches the post office and remove the money. Afterwards, when their messenger comes to the post-office box, we'll be waiting."

"Very well, gentlemen," said Hargrave, "we will, then, acting on your advice, follow out literally the instructions these scoundrels have given us." He got up from his chair and shook hands with the Commissioner.

"Of course, John," he suggested, "you will want a list from our bank of the serial numbers of the twenty-dollar bills?"

"As a matter of precaution," replied Mackay, "we might as well take them. But there will be no possibility of this money getting out of our hands. From the moment your man puts the package into the mail box on the corner of Sixth Avenue and Twenty-Eighth Street, until it is delivered to post office sub-station O, it will never be out of the possession of the Federal government or the police. I myself will wait at the post office and take the money in charge."

II

"HAVE ALL THE arrangements been made, Inspector?" inquired Hargrave anxiously.

"Yes, sir," Bullock replied. "Everything has been planned according to the Commissioner's orders. These two detectives here, Hawley and Dennis, will follow your messenger from the time he leaves your office until he arrives at the mail box. You can be sure the tailing will be done in such a manner that no one will know your man is being followed. These detectives will follow him to the mail box at Sixth Avenue and Twenty-Eighth Street, and after he has deposited the money in the box they have orders to wait until the postman has collected the mail at six-thirty P.M. Then they've been told to follow him and see that he is safely protected until he arrives at the post office."

After a few more minutes of conversation Mr. Hargrave sent for his head clerk who entered the room carrying in his hand a small satchel. This he placed on a desk, and opening it with great solemnity, began to count the thick pile of twenty-dollar bills. Then, assisted by his employer, he made a stout paper package of the currency. Mr. Hargrave thereupon affixed stamps and addressed the parcel to Harvey Jones, Box 817, U.S. Post Office Branch O, 112 West 18th Street, New York City.

Presently, when the package had been tied up and sealed with red wax, Mr. Hargrave turned to Bullock and said, "It's up to you now, Inspector."

Bullock nodded serenely and glanced at his watch. "Time to be going, boys," he told the two detectives. "We've got to put the package in the letter box at six o'clock and it's now nearly five-thirty."

Mr. Hargrave's head clerk had evidently already received his instructions for, without more ado, he put on his overcoat and hat, shoved the parcel deep into a pocket and walked out of the office. He descended in the elevator and stepped into a cab which was standing at the entrance of the building.

He waited for a moment until he saw the detectives enter the two taxis which had drawn up behind his own; then he tapped on the window and the driver started off.

With a deep sigh of relief, the head clerk leaned back against the leather cushion. Surely no harm could now befall either himself or his precious package. The driver of his taxi, he had been told, would be a police officer, and closely following were two of the crack members of the detective force.

His cab crept slowly up Broadway, occasionally turning into side streets in an abrupt manner, which several times threatened to throw Mr. Hargrave's messenger onto the floor. At first he was mystified by these strange peregrinations but it soon dawned on him that the driver was making these erratic evolutions in order to be doubly sure that the cab was not being followed.

The route uptown had evidently been carefully prearranged, for the two cars carrying the detectives had no difficulty in keeping the leading taxi in sight. Finally, when the driver of the first cab became satisfied that there was no pursuit, he cut back over to Lafayette Street, and drove rapidly northward. At Greeley Square he turned to the west and crossed slowly over toward Sixth Avenue.

The man with the package of money looked at his wrist watch; it was three minutes before six. Under the elevated railway a red light flickered; the taxi stopped in a line of cars, and its lone occupant dug his hand into his pocket, and grasped his package with moist fingers. Now that he was scarcely a block away from his destination, his fears, which up to this time had been lulled to sleep by the presence of the detectives, came acutely to the fore. Nervously he shifted about on the seat until the traffic lights changed and a policeman motioned the taxi on. The cab turned downtown, proceeded a scant one hundred yards and came to a stop alongside the letter box on the Twenty-Eighth Street corner. Mr. Hargrave's messenger took the package of money out of his pocket, opened the cab door, leaped out and pushed the parcel into the wide mouth of the mail box.

When this had been done, he stood on the curbing and energetically wiped his forehead with a damp handkerchief. He looked anxiously up and down Sixth Avenue but there were no signs of the following taxis.

This fancied lack of physical support seemed to have an immediate and frightening effect for he jumped into the cab and pounded vigorously on the window. The driver grinned back at him, changed gears and began to pick his way through the steady stream of traffic.

A few yards away the two detectives, Hawley and Dennis, were elbowing their way through the dense shopping throngs that eddied out of the numerous department stores of the district; but even though an onlooker might think that these two men were merely a small part of the untidy tide of homebound humanity, it was evident that one or the other of them was never far from the letter box in which rested Lucy Laverne's legacy.

III

Four blocks further up Sixth Avenue, Postman Billings, leather mail pouch slung over shoulder, was methodically covering his usual collection route. At the corner of Thirty-first Street he stopped before a mail box, inserted his key in the lock, shifted around the heavy bag, and stuffed a handful of letters into its capacious folds.

At the present moment his bag held but a scant dozen letters for he had just left the Greeley Square Post Office to begin his evening collection. He slammed shut the iron door of the mail box, and had just started to continue on his beat, when a window flew open on the second story of a nearby building and a man yelled, "Hi there, Postman. Here's a letter I've got to mail. I'll be right down with it."

Postman Billings walked across the sidewalk to the narrow entrance of the ancient brownstone house, opened the door and stepped inside. Hearing a clattering of feet on the next floor, he lifted his head to look up the stairs. As he did this, a man's figure emerged from behind the ramshackle stairway, tiptoed the few yards that removed him from Billings, raised his hand high in the air and crashed down a blackjack on the postman's skull with a sickening thud.

Without even a murmur the postman collapsed and lay in an inert heap on top of his mail bag.

His assailant whistled and at the signal another man came running from the floor above. Together the two carried Billings upstairs and stretched him out on a decrepit sofa.

Five minutes later a postman, whose suit didn't quite fit him, stepped out of the building which Billings had lately entered, walked down the street to the Twenty-Ninth Street mail box, opened it with his key and calmly dropped a few more letters into his pouch.

Presently he arrived at the mail box on Twenty-Eighth Street, where he went through a similar procedure; then he marched down the avenue followed at a discreet distance by the two wary detectives. Slowly and methodically the bogus postman cleaned out the boxes on the east side of the avenue; then he crossed over at Twenty-Fourth Street and started uptown, collecting mail as he went. At Thirty-Second Street he turned westward and walked briskly past the brightly glowing windows of Gimbel's. At Seventh Avenue he waited a moment on the corner until the traffic lights changed; then he hurried past the Pennsylvania Station toward the bulky General Post Office.

To the very doors of the post office, Hawley and Dennis followed their man; then as he passed through one of the many entrances the two detectives simultaneously reached into their pockets and lit up a pair of badly needed cigarettes.

"Well," said Dennis, between puffs, "that lets us out. The money's now safe in the hands of dear old Uncle Sam."

14
RIFTS IN THE CLOUDS

THE DOOR OPENED and detective Dennis and his partner entered the room. They stood meekly in front of the Commissioner while he glowered at them with complete disfavor and drummed his fingers fiercely on his desk.

"You can't pin it on us, sir," protested Dennis, the bolder of the two, who was a firm believer in the proverb that the best defence is offence. "Our instructions were to follow the postman from the box on the corner of Twenty-Eighth Street and Sixth Avenue until he had delivered the mail to the post office. This we did. How were we to know that the mail collected from that route should have been taken to the Greeley Square Post Office at 40 West Thirty-Second Street?"

The Commissioner viciously bit the end of his cigar. "I'm not blaming you," he exploded. "You did your best, I suppose—anyway you did what you were told to do. It's just one of those blasted things that would try the patience of fifty saints."

He turned to Bullock and prodded him in the ribs to emphasize his point. "These buzzards knew damn well we'd have the postman followed, and they were cute enough to prepare for it. After that fake mailman walked into the General Post Office building he had the pick of thirty or forty different doors to walk out of."

Mackay swung around toward the two detectives. "How about Billings, the postman?"

"He's got a nasty concussion," replied Dennis. "They've taken him to Bellevue. The ambulance surgeon didn't want him to talk so we couldn't get much out of him. He said he was hit from behind and didn't see who did it."

"And the building where he was attacked—what sort of place is it?" demanded the Commissioner.

"One of those tumbled-down brownstone houses. Full of Jewish fur dealers. As far as we can find out no one was working in the building when Billings was attacked, except an old man on the top floor who says he didn't hear anything."

Mackay drew a long breath and made an eloquent gesture of irritation. "That'll be all," he told Dennis and Hawley; the two withdrew in thankful alacrity.

"The really big question," pointed out Bullock, when the door closed behind the detectives, "is, will Lucy come back tomorrow?"

"She will not," stated John Mackay decisively. "*She's* got the money, and *we've* been given the bird. She's probably well out of the city by this time."

The Inspector shook his head in disagreement. "Not necessarily. I still think the girl was kidnapped. I don't believe she went away of her own free will."

"Well, tomorrow when she doesn't show up, you'll sing a different song," predicted the Commissioner. "You'll have to admit there'd be no reason for the kidnappers—if she *were* kidnapped—to keep her locked up after they'd been paid the fifty thousand dollars. After all, they couldn't get any more money out of the girl because I doubt very much if she has any more."

"That's true," replied Bullock, "but there's no use arguing; we'll find out tomorrow one way or the other."

The Commissioner began to pace nervously up and down the room.

"How about John McDonald?" inquired the Inspector.

"He ought to be here by this time," said Mackay looking at his watch, "and he isn't going to leave this building until I find out why he told you he hadn't seen Torrent on the Exchange the day of the murders. That's one lie he'll have a hard time explaining away."

Just then a policeman entered the office and announced that Mr. Jack McDonald was waiting outside; presently the broker was ushered in and the Commissioner motioned him toward a chair. McDonald seated himself and looked questioningly from Mackay to Bullock.

"May I ask," he requested, "the reason for this peremptory summons?"

Mackay abruptly shifted his cigar from the right corner of his mouth to the left. "Mr. McDonald," he replied coldly, "you told Inspector Bullock you were trading in General Electric stock at the close of the Exchange on Tuesday; we have reason to believe that statement is untrue. We've been informed that you were at the International Air-Conditioning post when the closing gong rang. What have you to say?"

"Plenty," returned the broker. "I said I was executing an order in General Electric, and that's where I was."

The Commissioner took out of his pocket a notecase and extracted a blue slip of paper. "I have here," he said, "the buy order which Philip Torrent executed just before the close. You will see that the last name he wrote was none other than yours. If he didn't trade with you, how do you account for this?"

Jack McDonald smiled serenely; there seemed to be no trace of fear on his face; instead, there was a distinct gleam of amusement in his eyes.

"May I see that order slip, Commissioner?"

Mackay handed over the blue piece of paper.

The broker glanced at the report; then passed it back. "I suppose this is what the Police call Exhibit A," he observed with a laugh. "If it is, I'll claim it as my own alibi."

"All right," snapped the Commissioner, "what's so funny?"

McDonald picked up the buy order once more, and held it in front of Mackay. "Do you see that little number 143 written underneath my name?"

"Sure," answered Bullock, "we saw it. We're not blind."

"Do you know what that number means?" persisted McDonald.

"No, I don't."

"Well, I'll tell you. Each member of the Exchange wears in the buttonhole of his coat a celluloid oval disk on which is printed his name, his firm's name and his number."

"Number?" queried Bullock.

"Yes," continued the broker. "To make it easy for members to identify each other during an active market every member has his own number. Sometimes, to save time while executing an order, we write down the man's number rather than his name."

"Well—so what?" demanded Bullock.

"Do you think," inquired McDonald, "that because Torrent had written on his report, 'bought 1000 IAC at 40½ from Jack McDonald,' that I must have been with him at Post No. 7 just before he collapsed?"

"That's our idea," admitted the Commissioner. "And we happen to know that your office delivered to the firm of Torrent & Hastings, one thousand shares of International Air-Conditioning stock the day after the murder."

McDonald shook his head impatiently. "See here, Mackay," he said, "I'm not denying Torrent bought that stock from me, but you will note that under the name Jack McDonald is the number 143."

"Yes."

"Well, my number happens to be 470."

The import of this information did not immediately become clear to the two policemen. They sat waiting for McDonald to continue his explanation. "143 is the number of my friend, Douglas Lake. As I told you I was busy with a large order in General Electric. Earlier in the day I had taken a flier in International Air-Conditioning and at the close of trading I asked Lake to sell the stock I had bought. He sold my thousand shares to Torrent and told him it was for my account. Torrent, as is the custom, put Lake's number under my name so that he could remember with whom he had actually traded."

II

Long after McDonald had left Police Headquarters Mackay and Bullock remained sitting in glum silence. A feeling of complete bafflement had gradually enveloped the two men. There were so many suspects in these murder cases; yet, time after time, the finger of suspicion had pointed determinedly at a certain person only to waver uncertainly before finally turning in an entirely different direction.

The telephone on Mackay's desk interrupted their moody reveries. The Commissioner took up the receiver.

"What!" he bellowed, when he had heard the message. "Lucy Laverne! Send her in! Send her in!"

He turned to Bullock and gesticulated excitedly. "She's outside."

"Well, I'll be damned," exclaimed the Inspector.

The door opened, and Lucy Laverne came into the room. She walked slowly over to the chair beside Mackay's desk. She sat down; then, losing her self-control completely, she burst into tears.

Bullock leaned over and patted her shoulder. "Now, now, Miss Laverne," he said consolingly, "tell us all about it."

The girl wiped her streaming eyes with a handkerchief. "Everything's too awful," she sobbed.

The tears continued to flow with unabated violence. Bullock and Mackay sat silent, waiting patiently for the girl to compose herself.

At last the story was told.

She had been walking down Fifty-First Street near Sixth Avenue, when a taxi had drawn up at the curb a few yards ahead, and a man alighted. As she came abreast of this man, he took out of his pocket a small revolver, and motioned her into the cab. Too excited and frightened to scream, she had meekly obeyed the command. Once she was in the taxi the man threatened her with instant death should she cry out or attempt to attract the attention of a policeman. She had been driven to an apartment house on One Hundred and Sixth Street where she had been forced to write the postscript on the ransom letter. Her lone abductor had kept her locked overnight in an almost soundproof closet, on the floor of which he had stretched a mattress. All the morning and afternoon he had stood guard over her. At five-thirty he put on his hat and coat, tied her to a chair and placed a small but efficient gag in her mouth. Around seven o'clock he had returned, unbound her hands and feet, and, telling her not to move for at least fifteen minutes, he went out of the apartment, leaving the hall door unlocked.

When she had finished her story, Mackay began his cross examination.

"Where'd you been just before this man held you up?"

"I was in a restaurant on Fifty-First Street."

"What for?"

"To have a cocktail."

"Are you sure?" demanded Mackay fiercely. "Sure you didn't go there to have a talk with Chipo Marinelli?"

The girl quivered in her chair as though she had been struck a physical blow.

"How'd you know?" she asked in a quavering voice.

The Commissioner ignored her question. "You'd better tell us the whole truth. It'll be better for you," he counseled.

Lucy Laverne dabbed at her reddened eyes, took out her vanity-case and powdered her nose.

"It's a long story," she said at last.

Bullock nodded encouragingly.

"To begin," she told them, "the lawyers said that because of large losses in Mr. Torrent's business I might not receive the money which he had left me in his will. They said that Mr. Torrent was not nearly as wealthy as everyone thought, and that several of his assets, including one item of seventy thousand dollars, were unaccounted for. Now I knew very well where that seventy thousand had gone, because, in the five years we were together, Mr. Torrent told me a great deal about his financial affairs. He had lent this money to Chipo Marinelli to buy a building and to open up a new and exclusive speak-easy. Several of his friends in Wall Street had put money into similar ventures and they had, in each case, received their money back and made large profits as well.

"You'll remember," she continued, "that 1931 was an exceptionally bad year for stock brokers and Mr. Torrent was very hard pressed to make any money in his business.

"When I heard I might not receive my legacy because Marinelli had not come forward to acknowledge his debt to Mr. Torrent, I naturally was very much agitated. I went to Marinelli, whom I've known for a long time, and I demanded that he communicate with

Hargrave, the executor of the estate, and make arrangements for repaying the money which he owed.

"We had a very long talk, and finally Marinelli offered me a proposition. He would give me immediately ten thousand dollars if I promised to tell no one about the money he owed Mr. Torrent; he also agreed that if there were any deficiency in my fifty-thousand-dollar legacy, he would make it good.

"As far as I could see I had ten thousand to gain and nothing to lose, so I accepted his offer and we parted on friendly terms."

Mackay clucked his tongue in shocked remonstrance. "That wasn't a very wise thing to do, Miss Laverne. Personally I'd call it just plain blackmail; in addition, you were depriving Mrs. Torrent of a very large sum of money."

"I'm not interested in Mrs. Torrent," replied Lucy Laverne callously. "She's the very least of my troubles."

The Commissioner stared for a moment out of one of the large old-fashioned windows of his office.

"Did it occur to you, Miss Laverne," he inquired, "that your friend Marinelli might have engineered your kidnapping?"

"Of course he didn't," she scoffed. "He couldn't have arranged such an affair so quickly."

"I wouldn't be too sure about that," answered Bullock grimly. "Did he have a chance to send a message or to telephone while you were talking to him?"

The girl puckered her eyebrows in perplexity. "Yes," she replied, "I think he did go up to his apartment on the top floor to attend to something."

"I very much think," said Mackay dryly, "that *that* something was you."

"Yes," chimed in Bullock. "I agree. He probably sent a message to some gangster friend while he was upstairs."

"Did he give you the ten thousand dollars he promised?" asked Mackay.

"Yes. I had it in my purse—in cash."

"Humph," observed Mackay. "So he got back his own ten thousand and your fifty thousand in addition. Don't you see how pretty he's sitting? If necessary he can now pay up most of the sum he owes Torrent's estate with your money, and the executors will say what an honest speak-easy proprietor he is."

The girl looked at the Commissioner with sceptical blue eyes. "It's a good theory, but I don't believe in it," she told him.

"Well, then," said Bullock, taking a different tack, "how about the fellow that kidnapped you? What'd he look like?"

"He was a stocky man with a large black mustache and very pink fat cheeks."

"That's a good description," applauded the Inspector. "Would you say he was a foreigner?"

"I don't think so. At least he had no accent."

"Would you recognize him again?"

"Oh, my, yes," replied Lucy Laverne. "I'd know him in a second."

Mackay reached across his desk and pushed one of a row of electric buttons. A policeman promptly appeared from the anteroom.

"Take this young lady down to the Identification Bureau, and tell Sergeant Baily to show her through our picture gallery."

He turned to Bullock. "Perhaps you'd better go along too, Inspector. You know the type of mugs that might be mixed up in a case like this."

III

TWO HOURS LATER Bullock rejoined the Commissioner.

"No luck," he announced. "Guess the fellow hasn't got a record."

Mackay shook his head dolefully. "You know, Inspector, I've been doing a lot of thinking during the last couple of hours about these Stock Exchange murders, and there's one peculiar angle to the cases that sticks in my crop. You very seldom hear of a murder where the poison that killed a man is known but the method of administration is unknown. Now, usually, you can say a murdered person died of eating poisoned food, or drinking poisoned liquor, or was hit over the head with an ax, or was smothered with a pillow; now in these two cases, we know they were murdered with curare, but how that poison got into their systems is still as much a mystery as it was on Tuesday afternoon.

"The Medical Examiner told us," continued Mackay, "that the poison entered the blood stream of these men through two small abrasions. In one case the cut is on the right ear, and in the other it's an inch or so below the left ear. Now, why should the places of entry be on, or near, the ear? There must be some significance in this fact, if we could only grasp it. If one is going to poison a man in that fashion, I should think it would be safer from the murderer's standpoint to introduce the poison into some lower part of the body."

"Most of the rest of the body is covered with clothes," pointed out Bullock. "All but the hands."

"Exactly," agreed his superior. "Consequently that implies to my mind that the weapon was not a hypodermic. If that had been used it could have easily penetrated a man's clothing."

"It certainly could," agreed Bullock.

Mackay continued with his thesis. "If then we discard the theory of death by injection, what have we left: that the scratch or cut on the ear was made either by a penknife or by some other pointed or sharp-edged instrument. Now, I don't think anyone could cut a man's ear with a penknife without ten or fifteen people seeing it done. We then come to the question of how the wound could be inflicted without attracting undue attention. Naturally, the only way this could be accomplished would be to use as an inoffensive weapon something so ordinary in appearance that no one would suspect that an ulterior use was being made of it."

The Inspector grunted in approval, and Mackay lit up one of his inevitable cigars. "What do *you* think is the commonest, most-used article on the Stock Exchange?" the Commissioner demanded.

"Brains?" inquired Bullock facetiously.

Mackay silenced him with a frown. "No, pencils."

"Oh, hell," retorted the Inspector. "We went all through that before. There wasn't a trace of poison on that red metal pencil we found on the floor."

"Quite true," admitted Mackay, "but if that needle-pointed pencil made the cuts, couldn't the poison have been administered afterwards?"

"But why go about it in such a roundabout way?" pointed out Bullock. "Why not just put the poison on the pencil tip?"

"I'm not a doctor, but I don't believe you could put enough curare on a phonograph needle to kill a grown man," replied the Commissioner. "I'm inclined to think that the pencil played a preliminary rather than a final part in our murder mystery.

"Now, since curare takes only about twenty minutes or so to kill, it's quite evident that the murderer was either a man who was on the Stock Exchange floor at the time or else it was Lucy Laverne who admits she called Torrent out to the lobby at about twenty minutes to three.

"According to Lucy's story," went on Mackay, "Chipo Marinelli had good reason to kill Torrent—to evade a repayment of the large amount of money the broker had lent him. On the other hand, I don't see how Marinelli could have possibly gotten onto the Exchange. As you know, it's the most heavily guarded place in the world, and sometimes even new members have trouble in being admitted until all the guards are familiar with their faces. This being so, I think we'll reluctantly have to rule Marinelli out of our list of suspects. That leaves Jack McDonald, Howard Torrent and Temple Hastings. They've all given us good cock-and-bull stories; but either or any of these men had the opportunity to kill both Philip Torrent and Sandy Harrison.

"Concerning these three men we have definitely ascertained the following facts: young Howard Torrent was familiar with the poison, curare, since he had attended a medical college; Temple Hastings was facing ruin and disgrace due to his partner's forthcoming complaint to the Stock Exchange authorities; Jack McDonald was held in the throes of a great love for Mary Torrent and when a man's in that condition he's liable to do anything."

"You said it, Chief," agreed Bullock. "Believe it or not I was once that way about a dame myself."

Bullock smiled broadly at his own joke and then as an afterthought said: "By the way, Commissioner, while we were downstairs, I asked Laverne about the hypodermic filled with insulin. She told me it belonged to a girl friend of hers who's suffering from diabetes. She said it was left in her apartment by mistake the day before yesterday."

"Did you check up on her statement?"

"Sure. I called this girl up. She said she's been telephoning Lucy for the last twenty-four hours, trying to get the hypo back. She said she'd come right down here and get it. She's supposed to take an injection of the stuff three times a day."

"Just another theory gone to hell," said Mackay resignedly. "Oh, well, we ought to be used to disappointments by now."

He yarned and inspected the crystal of his watch.

"Holy cats, it's almost eleven o'clock. We'd better be getting home. I've a feeling tomorrow's going to be a busy day."

IV

As the Brooklyn-bound subway train roared under the river, Bullock leaned his shoulders against the uncomfortable seat and quietly dozed off to sleep. The training acquired by long years of traveling back and forth in the subway had educated him to the point where he was able to awake just as he was arriving at his destination.

At the Flatbush Avenue station, he emerged into the cool night air and walked the three blocks that separated him from his home, the top floor of an old-fashioned, four-storied residence.

His wife, Maggie, had long since gone to bed, for she, conscientious soul, arose at an early hour in order to do her tidying-up, prepare the children for school and to see that the lord and master of the household departed with a contentedly full stomach.

The Inspector tiptoed down the hall, undressed in the dark, and slipped into the wide four-poster bed which was already more than adequately filled by Maggie.

He stared up at the black ceiling and a few memories of the events of the day came surging back.

Funny thing about the poison entering by the ear. Why on the ear? Why near both the men's ears? Why was one man poisoned on the left ear and the other on the right? Why? Why? Why?

He tossed about in the bed, tried vainly to go to sleep and finally gave the attempt up as a bad job.

For more than an hour he lay awake, his mind alert and questioning.

Suddenly he sat up in the bed, tossed the bedcovers aside and rushed toward the telephone in the adjoining room.

His wife, nearly startled to death, sleepily picked the sheets from off the floor and listened with growing bewilderment as he spoke to someone at Headquarters.

"Who's in charge tonight?" he demanded. "Who? Martin? Let me talk to him."

A moment later the connection was made. "Hello, hello, Bullock speaking. Do me a favor, will you? Send down and get out the photographs of the bodies of Harrison and Torrent. Yes, yes, the ones taken by the Homicide Squad's photographer just as they were found."

There was a four-minute silence while the pictures were being procured.

"I've got them now," announced Inspector Martin over the wire. "What do you want?"

"Look at the pictures of Harrison," demanded Bullock. "Can you see his wrist watch?"

"Sure," replied Martin jovially. "Do you want to know what time it says—you old Sherlock Holmes?"

"Which wrist is the watch on?" asked Bullock eagerly.

"On the right wrist."

"Thanks," was the reply. "That's all."

Inspector Martin hung up, half doubting in his own mind his colleague's sanity.

If he could have seen Bullock actually skipping back to his bedroom his doubt would have been turned to certainty.

But Bullock had every right to skip for at last he had discovered how the murders had been committed.

15
THE PERFECT ALIBI

Bullock slept very little for the remainder of the night; at seven he had finished his breakfast, and at eight-thirty he was in the Stock Exchange building, waiting for his friend Barton, the assistant secretary, to arrive from the suburbs.

On his way to the Exchange, the Inspector stopped momentarily at Headquarters and gathered up a few of the clues that had been found on the Exchange Floor—namely, the red-metal pencil, the note from McDonald to Torrent concerning their luncheon engagement, the buy orders of *Torrent & Hastings*, the one order slip of *Harrison & McGuire* and the two message blanks notifying Torrent he was wanted on the telephone. Added to these, the Inspector carefully placed in a large brown envelope the two wrist watches that had been found on the murdered men, and the blood-spotted handkerchiefs which had been taken from their pockets.

At nine o'clock Barton arrived, to be informed that Bullock was desirous of going down once more to the Stock Exchange.

Soon the two men were walking across the practically deserted Floor in the direction of the smoking room.

"First of all," said Bullock, "I want to go to the members' main telephone exchange."

Barton led him to a near-by room in the middle of which was a large switchboard where two page boys were already in attendance. On one side of the room was a long row of booths.

Bullock walked into booth number twelve, took out his penknife and promptly cut the cord that connected the receiver to the telephone.

He stepped out of the booth, holding the severed end of the wire. "Now, if *you* did that I'd have you arrested," he told Barton with a grin.

Barton's eyes were popping out with astonishment and he seemed to have entirely lost the power of speech.

"This phone can be fixed, can't it?" inquired Bullock. "I'd like to take this catch with me." He swung the receiver to and fro as though it were a fat fish on the end of a line.

"Oh, yes. It can be repaired immediately," the assistant secretary finally answered, when he had recovered from his amazement. "There are more than three thousand telephones on the Exchange Floor and the New York Telephone Company keeps a special staff of men here to look after them."

"Fine," said the Inspector. "Then I haven't done a great deal of damage. And now, where's the 18 Broad Street entrance?"

Barton showed the way, and a minute later Bullock entered one of the booths that stood near the door, and repeated his act of vandalism.

He then wrapped the receivers in two pieces of paper, writing on the outside of one, "Main telephone exchange—Booth 12," and on the other, "Booth 4—18 Broad Street entrance."

Afterwards, he ceremoniously thanked Barton for his assistance, and departed, leaving his late companion in a state of annoyed mystification.

Once more he drove up the rocky Avenue A to the Chief Medical Examiner's offices. Once more he sat and enjoyed Dr. Moss's excellent bourbon while the telephone receivers were being dispatched to the laboratory.

"You must think," observed Dr. Moss jovially, "that I have nothing to do but work for you. If something doesn't come of this analysis I'm going to go on strike."

A half hour later the head pathologist came into the room and handed his chief the report of his investigation.

"The result of the analysis is as follows," read the Doctor. "We have found no signs of curare on the telephone receiver marked 'Main telephone exchange—Booth 12'; we have found no signs of curare on the exterior of the receiver marked '18 Broad Street—Booth 4—'"

The Inspector gave a groan of disappointment.

"We have, however," continued Dr. Moss imperturbably, "found distinct traces of curare on the sounding diaphragm of the Broad Street receiver."

Bullock leapt out of his chair with a hoarse cheer of triumph.

II

"Of course," pointed out Bullock, "there could hardly be any trace of the poison on the disk end of the telephone receivers. It's been seventy-two hours since the murder, and at least a hundred different people have pressed that receiver against their ears since then. The only place any curare could possibly remain was in the diaphragm—the little hole in the base of the receiver."

"This discovery of yours," observed Mackay, "unfortunately adds a great many more complications to the case. Previously we've been convinced that the murderer was actually on the Exchange when the crimes were committed; now it looks as though the murderer made his plans, left the Exchange and then called his victims to the telephone."

"That's true up to a certain point," admitted Bullock. "I think we might be certain that the red metal pencil tipped by the phonograph needle was used to scratch Torrent's ear just before he went to the telephone. Now such a small, superficial cut heals very quickly; therefore, the person who telephoned Torrent must had had an accomplice on the Floor who knew exactly when the telephone call was to be made, and that person scratched Torrent's ear, at an appointed time. If this had been done too soon, the wound would have healed and the poison spread on the base of the telephone receiver wouldn't have gotten into the blood stream."

"You're quite correct, Inspector," approved the Commissioner, "you've made that part very clear; but now, tell me, what was the second and more important discovery you spoke of?"

"Do you remember, sir," began Bullock, "that a day or so ago we were talking about the 'common denominator,' and we both agreed that until we found the link between these two deaths we wouldn't get anywhere?"

"Certainly," replied Mackay, "I remember our conversation distinctly."

The Inspector hitched his chair closer to his superior and said in a dramatic voice, "There isn't any 'common denominator'; these two men met their deaths for entirely different reasons and to all practical purposes were killed by different hands."

"What," exclaimed Mackay, dumfounded. "Different people killed them with the same poison?"

"Exactly," insisted Bullock. "I haven't any idea who killed Torrent, but the person responsible for Sandy Harrison's death was Lucy Laverne."

"You can prove this?" almost shouted the Commissioner.

"Certainly. The person who murdered Torrent placed the curare on the telephone receiver in booth number four at the Broad Street entrance. Then he, or an accomplice, after cutting Torrent's ear, had him called to that booth. There's no switchboard at that set of booths; each phone has its own individual number, so it would be a simple matter to call Torrent to the poisoned telephone. When Torrent arrived to receive the message he picked up the receiver, placed it against his ear and the poison immediately entered through the cut on his right ear."

"All very well," replied Mackay, "but Harrison died as the result of an infection on the left side of the face, so how could he have been poisoned?" He turned challengingly to the Inspector. "How about that?"

"Sandy Harrison would have been alive today," promptly replied Bullock, "except for the fact that he had the exceedingly bad luck to be left handed."

"Left handed?" inquired his superior blankly. "What's that got to do with it?"

"Lucy Laverne's nail scratches were on the left side of his face just below his ear. Unfortunately, he went into booth number four to make a telephone call, and, since he was left handed, he put the receiver to his left ear. The scratch marks of Lucy's finger nails just beneath his ear were still raw—perhaps like most of us with a half-healed scab he could not resist the temptation to finger the wound. The blood stains we found on his handkerchief plainly show that the abrasions had started to bleed once more."

"So Sandy's death was an accident," said the Commissioner, regarding Bullock with undisguised approval. "I've got to hand it to you, Inspector. The whole thing sounds like the work of one of your pals in the mystery books."

Bullock lifted his hands as though to ward off a blow. "Not that!" he pleaded earnestly.

Mackay became serious once more. "How'd you discover Harrison was left handed?"

"By his wrist watch," answered Bullock. "He wore it on his right wrist. Almost invariably a right-handed man wears his watch on his left wrist and vice versa. The idea is you put it on the arm you use the least. This morning I telephoned his secretary and checked up. He was left handed all right."

Mackay squirmed uneasily about in his chair. "Of course," he observed, "it's fine detective work, but it doesn't help us any. We still don't know who murdered Torrent; and in some respects, all this, instead of lessening our list of potential murders, increases them. Previously, we have suspected only the people who were on the Exchange—young Howard Torrent, John McDonald and Temple Hastings; but now, according to your theory, the real murderer was the person who telephoned to booth number four and asked to speak to Torrent."

Bullock nodded sourly. "I've thought of that, too, Chief. And the worst of it is that it brings the dames in again. Lucy Laverne told us she telephoned Torrent, just before she came to call on him at two-forty, and Mrs. Torrent said she phoned him from her lawyer's office at about the same time. On top of that we have the telephone notification slip saying that Chipo Marinelli wanted to speak to him. Of course, we don't know exactly when Marinelli called but it might have been around two-thirty also."

"That's all very true," assented Mackay, "but I think you yourself have not appreciated all the ramifications of your discovery.

According to your theory, someone on the Exchange used the red metal pencil to scratch Torrent's ear. There's no doubt in my mind that that is precisely what happened. The lamp black or soot was put on the phonograph needle to make it look exactly like a pencil point. In the excitement of the trading in International Air-Conditioning, Torrent would probably not feel the slight scratch on his ear, particularly if he were engrossed in the execution of a large order. With twenty or more men milling about, shouting and waving their hands in the air, it would be the simplest matter in the world to cut his ear without anyone being the wiser."

"However," Mackay continued, "there's another angle: Howard Torrent or Jack McDonald or Temple Hastings could have placed the curare on the telephone, but neither Howard Torrent nor Jack McDonald nor Temple Hastings could have attacked Philip Torrent with the metal pencil."

"I don't get you," objected Bullock. "How d'ye figure that out?"

"In this way," replied his superior. "Philip Torrent first showed signs of poisoning at about three minutes after three. Dr. Moss told us that curare took effect in about twenty minutes; therefore Torrent must have gone to the telephone approximately twenty minutes before three, and by the same reckoning his ear must have been scratched a minute or so before that.

"Now where was Jack McDonald at about that time? He told us he was in the General Electric crowd, executing a large order. In order to check up on his statement I telephoned the specialist in that stock this morning and he assured me that McDonald had told the truth. He also volunteered the information that McDonald had remained at the General Electric post from about two-fifteen until the close. This gives him an iron-clad alibi as far as the pencil part of the murder is concerned.

"Now, where was young Howard Torrent? He was busier than a one-armed paperhanger, keeping his employer's books up to the minute in a boiling market. In addition he was surrounded by seven or eight other clerks who saw his every movement, and, as if these weren't sufficient alibis, there is the further fact that clerks are not allowed out on the Floor during trading hours.

"Now where was Temple Hastings? He had remained in the Stock Exchange Luncheon Club until after two-thirty; then in a half soused state he went down to the Exchange. Logan, an ex-policeman, who is one of the guards at the lobby entrance, told me that Hastings went by him onto the Floor at about fifteen minutes before three. Considering his drunken condition and the lateness of the hour I don't think it likely that he murdered Torrent. This crime was not committed by a drunken person; it was far too cleverly worked out for that."

The Inspector remained silent for more than a minute and carefully digested Mackay's words. "Well," he observed finally, "I hope you're satisfied. You've given almost everybody a fine alibi. Who in hell is left to suspect?"

"We've still got a few," pointed out the Commissioner with a smile. "There's Lucy Laverne, and Mary Torrent, and Chipo Marinelli."

"Pshaw!" was Bullock's bitter reply. "Those girls couldn't get on the Exchange and neither could Marinelli." He paused and a thoughtful look came into his eye. "By the way, Chief, we haven't found out what time Marinelli telephoned to Torrent, and I haven't had time to ask him about Laverne's kidnapping. I think I'll take a run uptown and have a few words with that baby."

III

Bullock walked into the dining-room of Marinelli's restaurant and seated himself comfortably at a table. "I'm getting to be quite a customer of yours," he told the Italian.

"A non-paying one," commented the proprietor without rancor.

The Inspector laughed good-naturedly. "I'll promise to pay from now on," he said. "What'll you have?"

The waiter brought drinks and placed them between the two men.

"Figli Moschi," proposed the Italian. Together they took their first sips.

"I suppose you heard about Lucy Laverne?" inquired Bullock casually, after setting down his half-emptied glass.

"No. What about her?"

"She was kidnapped."

"What!" exclaimed Marinelli. Astonishment was written all over his face. "When?"

"Yesterday," replied the Inspector. "Just after she left you," he added dryly.

"Have they let her go?" asked Marinelli.

"Yes. That's what I'm here for. She seems to think you've got something to do with it."

"That's a damn lie," hotly retorted the Italian.

Bullock flicked the ash of his cigarette onto the floor. "Maybe," he replied non-committedly. "Anyhow she told us about the convenient little arrangement she made with you."

Marinelli's face grew sullen. "You'd have done the same thing yourself. I didn't want to pay back all that money."

"What're you going to do about it?" demanded the Inspector.

"It's none of your damn business what I do about it. I know my rights—it's a civil case. If they want the money, all they have to do is sue me."

The Inspector, who knew only too well the truth of this assertion, wisely kept his temper.

"And if they win, you'll pay up? How? What with?" he blandly inquired.

"That's my business, but I can get the dough if I have to."

Bullock calmly drained the remainder of his old- fashioned cocktail, and looked about the room.

"What's all the decorations for?" he asked, pointing at the walls which were bedecked with colored streamers.

"I'm giving a party tonight. It's my tenth wedding anniversary," explained Marinelli. "All my wife's relations are coming." He added with a shrug, "She's got a million of them."

"Did you get married in Italy?" inquired Bullock by way of making conversation. He was determined to keep his interview with thc Italian on a friendly basis.

"No," answered Marinelli, "down at the City Hall."

The Inspector called for another round of drinks and proceeded cautiously to find out about the telephone call.

"You told me a couple of days ago that you telephoned Mr. Torrent on Tuesday to ask him to go bail for you—that's right, isn't it?"

"Yes," replied the Italian shortly.

"What time was that?"

"About ten-thirty. The cops let me phone him before they took me to jail."

"You only called him once?"

"Yes."

"You're sure you didn't call him again around two-thirty?"

"Sure, I'm sure. I couldn't have called him at two-thirty because from eleven o'clock until four I was locked up in one of your sweet airy cells in the 18th Precinct Station House."

16
A LESSON IN GEOGRAPHY

"The more I think of it, the more I'm convinced there must have been two persons responsible for this murder," stated Bullock, who had returned to Headquarters to report to the Commissioner. "None of the people we suspect could have put the curare on the telephone, cut Torrent's ear and also called him to the phone without assistance."

Mackay's only reply was an approving nod of the head.

"Now what *pair* have we that might conceivably have worked together?" Bullock paused for a moment, then answered his own question. "There's Mary Torrent and Jack McDonald. They come automatically to mind for they're the most obviously linked couple. Then, there's Howard Torrent and Temple Hastings. Although we haven't been able to find the least connection between them it's not beyond the realms of possibility that they plotted the murder together. That leaves Chipo Marinelli and Lucy Laverne. Could they be the murderers? Hardly, because neither of them could have been the person on the Exchange Floor. How about Marinelli and Temple Hastings? That sounds more plausible. Marinelli told me he'd known Hastings for some years, and since both these men had been cheating and robbing Torrent this common tie might easily have led them into planning the murder."

The Commissioner thoughtfully chewed on the stub of his cigar. "Well, while you're talking about couples—how about Chipo and his wife Maria?"

"I've thought of them, sir," answered Bullock. "But the idea doesn't jell. Of the two persons who committed the murder—if there *were* two—one must have been on the Stock Exchange at the time of, or at the least just before, the murder. Chipo was in jail, and Maria certainly wasn't on the Exchange, and I—"

"You know," interrupted the Commissioner, "we've done a lot of speculating about 'who' and 'why' in this case, but we haven't paid as much attention to 'how.' Now curare is a damned unusual poison. It's all very well to say that Howard Torrent, having studied medicine, would know about it, but as far as I can see we've about eliminated that young man from our list of suspects. Obviously someone else on the Exchange was familiar with curare. Who would that be? The most obvious answer is—someone who'd been in the countries where the weed, that this poison is derived from, grows.

"Now, I don't suppose Chipo's been in the wilds of South America, nor does it seem likely that hothouse creatures such as Mary Torrent or Lucy Laverne would be familiar with those regions; but Temple Hastings or Jack McDonald might easily have been there. Both men were rich, and very probably had traveled extensively."

"That's true," agreed Bullock. "How about trying to find out if either of them has ever been in Brazil or Paraguay? I'll call up McDonald and ask him. He'd hardly dare lie because it'd be a simple matter for us to check on him."

The Inspector picked up the telephone and called the Stock Exchange. After a five minutes' wait, Jack McDonald answered and Bullock bluntly inquired: "Have you ever been in Brazil or Paraguay?"

There was a moment's silence; then the broker replied, "I've been in Brazil."

"When was that?"

"About a year ago. I went on a South American cruise. We touched at several ports in Brazil."

"How long did you stay at Rio?"

"Three days."

"Thank you very much, Mr. McDonald," said Bullock silkily. "That'll be all."

He turned to Mackay. "Of course it doesn't necessarily mean anything. Brazil's a big country—bigger even than the United States and lots of people go there. But he *might* have brought some curare back with him."

"Find out about Hastings," directed the Commissioner.

A telephone call to Hastings' office elicited the information that the broker was out of town. Bullock was just about to ring off when he remembered Miss Snowden, Torrent's secretary.

A moment later he was talking to her.

"Oh, yes," she replied in answer to his question. "Mr. Hastings has been in both Brazil and Paraguay. He spent six years in South America before he went into the brokerage business. I've often heard him tell of his adventures. He stayed a long while in Brazil prospecting for gold."

"Has he been in South America lately?"

"Not since I've been with the firm. And that's over eight years," answered the girl, "but he owns property down there."

"Where?" demanded the Inspector.

"He has a maté plantation in Paraguay, on the banks of the Pilcomayo River."

After a few more questions, which brought out nothing further of interest, Bullock thanked Miss Snowden and hung up.

"For the love of Mike, what's maté?" he demanded.

"Search me," answered Mackay truthfully. "Maybe it's the stuff they make mattresses out of," he added with a smile.

He pushed one of the electric buttons on the desk in front of him. "It seems to me," he observed to Bullock, "that we don't know much about Paraguay. Let's find out a thing or two."

A policeman knocked on the door in answer to the summons and Mackay bade him enter.

"Go down to the Reference Library and bring me the volume of the Encyclopedia Britannica which tells about Paraguay," the Commissioner instructed him.

After the man had departed on his errand, Bullock told his superior, "I suppose it's a dumb thing to admit, but if you gave me ten dollars this minute I couldn't tell you exactly where Paraguay is. That is, I couldn't tell you what countries were on either side of it."

"Don't ask me," the Commissioner advised. "You know as much about the place as I do. All I know is that they're having a war down there. It's near Venezuela, I think."

The policeman soon returned with the desired volume and the two men began to pore over the four, closely written pages of information.

"It's nowhere near Venezuela," the Inspector remarked with a trace of malice after he had read a few paragraphs. "It's bounded on the northwest by Bolivia, the northeast by Brazil, and the south by Argentina."

Mackay ignored the subtle dig, and began to read out loud:

"'The two principal rivers are the Pilcomayo and the river Paraguay; the latter running from north to south divides the republic into two sections, the eastern section or Paraguay Oriental being the most important.'"

He skipped a few lines and began reading again. "'The two seasons of the year are divided thus: summer being from October to March and winter from April to September.'"

Bullock who had been looking at the facing page interrupted. "Here's all about maté. It's something like tea. It's one of their largest exports and it's widely used in Argentina in place of Brazilian coffee on which there's a heavy tax."

"Do you see anything more about the river Pilcomayo where Hastings has his mate plantation?"

"Nothing much. It just says that the river Pilcomayo runs through some of the wildest districts of Paraguay which are inhabited almost exclusively by Guarani Indians."

"Aren't those the hospitable little souls who use curare to poison their arrows?" demanded Mackay. "I think that's the tribe the Chief Medical Examiner told us about."

"It certainly is," agreed the Inspector, "and here's what the Encyclopedia has to say about curare. 'Curare, an arrow poison, may be swallowed in considerable quantity without appreciable result, whilst a minute quantity of the same substance introduced into a wound is speedily fatal.'"

"I think," observed Mackay, "that we'd better have another interview with our friend Temple Hastings. If I'd known he had property rights in the middle of what we might call the curare belt, he'd have had to do a lot more explaining than he did."

Bullock nodded in reply. His eyes were straying down the last page of Paraguayan descriptive matter.

Suddenly he gave an excited shout and grasped the Encyclopedia as though fearful lest someone should snatch it from him.

"What's biting you?" demanded Mackay, looking curiously at Bullock who was staring with transfixed eyes at a short sentence in the middle of the page.

"Don't ask me!" ejaculated the Inspector. "It's too good to be true! If you pinch me I'll wake up sure!"

"Horses!" replied the Commissioner inelegantly. "What do you see in there?"

Bullock shook his head decisively. "Give me a half hour, Chief," he pleaded. "Then I'll tell you. If my hunch is right, the murder is solved; if it isn't, I'm just a damn fool."

II

BULLOCK RUSHED OUT of the dingy, red stone Headquarters' building and walked rapidly down Lafayette Street.

As he hurried southward his head swam dizzily with the excitement of his discovery. How obvious the whole thing seemed now after he had seen by chance a few words in the Encyclopedia! But stop, he said to himself. Best not to be too hasty. Birds almost in the hand, he had discovered from long years of police work, had a habit of flying out of the bush.

He marched briskly past the chaste Grecian exterior of the New York County Court House, and entered the towering Municipal Building; he then took an elevator, and, with the air of one quite familiar with his surroundings, ordered the operator to drop him off at a certain floor.

On arrival there, he walked down a wide corridor until he came face to face with an impressive brass door marked "Marriage License Bureau, Chief Clerk's Office."

He gave his name to a clerk who met him in the anteroom, and seated himself in a large, bare room that was already filled to overflowing by a throng of bashful would-be brides and grooms.

The clerk returned to tell Bullock that his friend the Chief Clerk would be busy for fifteen or twenty minutes; and the Inspector, on receiving this information, picked up a newspaper from a table in the center of the room and made himself comfortable on a leather-backed couch.

The paper, like a magazine in a dentist's office, was not of the very latest vintage. In point of fact it was a Sunday *American* more than three weeks old; but Bullock turned the pages to the desired portion with the deliberation of a Sunday supplement connoisseur.

On the magazine section he found numerous items of passing interest.

On page two there was:

KIDNAPPING—THE NEW NATIONAL MENACE.

There he read, with quiet amusement, the stirring remarks of the Chief of Police of a small mid-western town who boldly advocated the immediate lynching of apprehended kidnappers.

On page three:

THE END OF THE BREACH-OF-PROMISE RACKET.

Here he was told by Federal Judge John Sylvester Tyler that either from the effects of the late depression or for some other reasons, which the Judge tried unsuccessfully to explain, juries were showing a most astounding increase in intelligence, and were firmly denying to the broken-hearted the soothing poultices of juicy cash settlements.

On the following page, Bullock found:

WHY JUNE BUGS HAVE NO SENSE OF DIRECTION.

But, since he had no interest either in June bugs or their sense of direction, he turned to the next article, which had been written by the famous Professor Heinrich Molvani, the distinguished Berlin physician:

WHAT SCIENCE HAS LEARNED ABOUT PLURAL BIRTHS.

Bullock had read about half of the Professor's theories, when he received a message informing him that his friend, the Chief Clerk, was now disengaged.

The Inspector folded up the newspaper and thrust it into his pocket for future perusal. A moment later he was shaking hands with Tom McManus, the genial white-haired man who had launched so many connubial barks on the troubled sea of matrimony.

"Well, well," greeted McManus, "if it isn't the old super-sleuth himself. What have you come for —a marriage license?"

The Inspector ignored the Chief Clerk's levity. "How many people a day do you marry here, Tom?" he asked abruptly.

"It all depends on the season of the year," replied McManus. "You know—'in the spring a young man's fancy—'"

"I know, I know," answered Bullock testily. "But about how many on an average?"

"Anywhere from twenty-five to a hundred."

"Where do you keep the records of these marriages?"

"Down in the sub-cellars of this building," McManus replied.

"Would it be difficult to get out some of your old records," persisted Bullock.

"Inconvenient perhaps," admitted McManus, "but not particularly difficult."

"Well, then," said Bullock, "I'd like to see a list of all the people that were married here on April 4th, 1925."

17
UNINVITED GUESTS

BULLOCK WALKED OVER to Park Row, hailed a taxi and directed the cabby to drive him to the Stock Exchange. On the way downtown he took from his pocket the Sunday *American* and finished reading the article he had begun at the License Bureau; then, he settled back into a corner of the cab, and a dreamy look of anticipation came into his eyes.

Arriving at the Exchange, he went straight to Barton's office, and, luckily finding him unoccupied by any pressing duties, Bullock took him by the arm and led him down to the Floor.

"I think we'll make a broker out of you yet," the assistant secretary chaffed. "You seem to like this noisy little room of ours. This is the third or fourth time you've been on the Floor."

"And it'll be the last time, I hope," Bullock answered. "I've got a feeling this case is soon going to be busted wide open."

"I sincerely hope so," said Barton. "In the last two days I've begun to fear you'd never find the murderer, and as for the newspapers—"

Bullock interrupted him violently. "Don't talk to me about *them*. They always love to pick on us, but they're certainly excelling their previous record in panning us about these so-called 'Stock Exchange Murders.'"

The Inspector changed the highly distasteful subject and inquired, "What was the name of that page boy who was working at the main switchboard the day Torrent was murdered—I mean the boy with the bad handwriting?"

"His name is Henry Thompson," replied the assistant secretary.

"Where is he now?" demanded Bullock.

"He's still at the telephones, I presume," replied his companion. "If they're efficient at the switchboard we generally leave them there. Usually boys haven't got enough patience; that's the reason the Telephone Company always employs girls for similar jobs."

Barton led the way through turbulent crowds of brokers; every foot or so the two men had to dodge to escape an impact with hurrying gray-clad pages, and in consequence their progress across the Floor was a slow succession of stops and starts.

Finally, arriving at the smoking room, where numerous brokers were enlivening a quiet minute or two with games of backgammon, they passed into the telephone room, and Barton pointed out one of the two boys who sat behind the switchboard. "That's Henry Thompson."

Bullock walked over to the boy. "I'm Inspector Bullock," he explained. "I'm making a few more inquiries about the murders." He beamed paternally down on the page. "Mr. Barton tells me you received a call for Mr. Torrent on Tuesday from a man named Marinelli. Do you remember the call?"

"Yes, sir," replied the boy promptly. "I remember it distinctly."

"At what time did the call come through?"

"It was about eleven, I think; or perhaps a little earlier. I know it was before eleven-fifteen, because I go to lunch at that time."

"Eleven fifteen lunch?" inquired Bullock. "Isn't that a bit early?"

"Yes, sir," the page answered with a side glance at Barton. "It's a funny hour, but we have to spread our lunch time so there'll always be enough boys on the Floor."

"I see," said the Inspector. "Now, when did you return to your switchboard?"

"At eleven forty-five."

"Do you remember any calls for Mr. Torrent after that hour?"

"No, sir. There were no more calls here, but he might have received messages through any of the booths nearer the Floor."

Bullock nodded encouragingly and the boy continued with his explanation. "You know, sir, very few brokers use this switchboard except for long distance calls. Most of them use the ordinary booths where there's no operator who might listen to their conversation. It's remarkable the number of ladies most brokers have to talk to."

Barton had a shocked expression on his face, but Bullock smiled understandingly. "So I've heard somewhere," he replied, very seriously, "in a fairy story, I think."

He grinned so broadly at the assistant secretary that even Barton's wooden face became wreathed in smiles.

He patted the page boy benevolently on the back. "You keep on being observant," he told him, "and maybe some day you'll grow up to be a broker and have beautiful ladies telephoning you all day long."

"And now," he said to Barton, "I want to find out a little more about these bright young employees of yours. Who has charge of them? It must be a hell of a job!"

"The personnel department is the place for you," the assistant secretary said. "All the records concerning our boys are kept up there."

"Lead the way," directed Bullock.

Presently they arrived at a large, bustling suite of offices, and Barton introduced the Inspector to Mr. Tate, the personnel director.

When this formality had been accomplished, Barton excused himself, and, saying that he had duties which demanded his attention, he consigned the Inspector to the good graces of Mr. Tate, who promptly made Bullock very much at home and presented him with a most excellent cigar.

"What I'd like to see first, Mr. Tate," the Inspector pointed out after lighting up his cigar, "is a list of your employees."

"You mean every employee of the Exchange?" demanded the personnel director. "That's a pretty large order."

"I know it is; but that's what I want—clerks, telephone boys, guards, pages, statisticians, economists and whatever else you've got—I'd like to look at their records."

"Fortunately," replied Mr. Tate, "that will be very simple. We pride ourselves on the exact check we keep on all our employees.

In the first place, we consider it an honor to work for the Exchange, and the boys and men in its service must measure up to a very high standard of behavior; secondly, since we act in a fiduciary capacity to the public, we reserve to ourselves the right to supervise the private lives of our employees if it becomes necessary. For instance, if it comes to our notice that one of our boys is associating with people of questionable character, he is told that this state of affairs must cease."

"Fine," applauded the Inspector. "But where are the records?"

Mr. Tate led him over to a battery of filing cabinets. "You'll find everything in here."

Although Bullock had told the personnel director that he wanted to see the dossiers of everyone in the Exchange's employ, he did not take more than five minutes to complete his investigation, and he was soon bidding goodbye to Mr. Tate.

He took the elevator down to the Stock Exchange building lobby, and giving a cheery hello to his friend Logan, walked once more onto the Floor.

With the air of one who has long since decided on the proper course of action, he made his way toward the telephone exchange. Young Henry Thompson was still seated at his switchboard, busily engaged in getting through a Chicago message. Bullock leaned his arm negligently on the top of the switchboard, and waited patiently for an opportunity to engage the boy in a few moments of conversation. Finally his chance came.

"Do you want to ask me some more questions?" asked Thompson.

"Just a few," Bullock told him. "The first is, do you know a page named Rivers?"

"Yes, sir, I sure do. He's one of my best friends."

"Does he also attend to telephones?" demanded the Inspector.

"No, sir. He's one of the Floor pages. Takes orders out to brokers and that sort of thing."

"Is he stationed near Post 7?" persisted Bullock.

"I'm not sure where he's stationed now, but he used to be somewhere in that vicinity."

"I suppose you could get in touch with that boy. I've a few questions to ask him. If he was near Post 7 on Tuesday, he may have seen something I'm anxious to check up on."

"I can get him for you right away," said Thompson. He spoke to another page boy, who hurried off to return almost immediately with a handsome, dark-haired young man.

"Your name is George Rivers?" inquired the Inspector.

"Yes, sir."

Bullock stared long and searchingly at the page, then he said, "Young Thompson, here, tells me you're stationed near the Air-Conditioning crowd."

"That's correct, sir."

"In that case you may have seen something on Tuesday that might—"

"I'm sorry, sir, I'm afraid not."

Bullock looked keenly at the boy. "What d'ye mean," he demanded.

"I wasn't here on Tuesday," the youth explained. "I was sick and had to remain in bed almost the entire day."

"Oh," replied Bullock in a peculiar voice. From his intonation one would have been hard put to decide whether this bit of information was agreeable or disagreeable to him. "Then I'm afraid I'm wasting both my time and yours. Obviously if you weren't here on Tuesday you couldn't tell me anything that has any bearing on the murder."

He smiled genially and waved his hand in a vague gesture of dismissal.

II

THREE HOURS LATER at Headquarters, a tense undercurrent of excitement disturbed the calm of systematic routine. In the Commissioner's private office, Bullock and Mackay sat in a corner of the room, mysteriously whispering as though fearful lest there be eavesdroppers even in this holy of holies.

Some minutes earlier, Mulligan had been dispatched with such strict and implicit instructions as to what he should and should not do, that his head spun dizzily as he strove to remember them all. Near the door stood Detectives Logan and Hawley, still smarting from the ignominy engendered by the trickery of the bogus postman. There was a stern expression on their stolid faces.

The Commissioner, concluding his conference with Bullock, called the two detectives to his side. "Men," he said, "this has been a hell of a case—the hardest nut to crack since I've been in office. But thanks to Inspector Bullock, we now know who the murderer is. In a few minutes, you're going after this bird, and I'm going with you."

Mackay rose from his chair and pointed an admonishing finger at the detectives. "Keep your guns handy—we'll probably need them!"

With these words the Commissioner put on his overcoat and hat, and walked down the corridor to the elevator; the Inspector, Dennis and Hawley followed closely behind.

On Centre Street, Mackay's car stood waiting, a burly policeman dressed in an ordinary chauffeur's uniform sitting at the wheel. Hawley climbed in beside the driver, while the Commissioner, Bullock and Dennis occupied the tonneau of the car. The chauffeur had already received his instructions, for he started off immediately and drove rapidly uptown.

The long black and silver automobile was a familiar object to traffic officers at the street intersections, and they waved Mackay along with a fine disregard for crosstown vehicles. In less than fifteen minutes they had reached Forty-Second Street, and a few minutes later the car came to a stop a hundred feet from Chipo Marinelli's restaurant.

"Let me go in first," said Bullock to the Commissioner. "The doorman knows me, and he'll admit me without question. If he sees a crowd of us he probably won't let us in."

Mackay nodded approvingly and the Inspector walked up to the entrance and pressed the bell.

The doorman peered through the iron grille, recognized the visitor and swung the door open.

Bullock, who had been standing in a negligent attitude with one hand behind his back, suddenly prodded the man's ribs with the barrel of his revolver.

"Not a peep out of you!" he commanded grimly.

The Commissioner and the two detectives, who had remained seated in the automobile, quickly joined Bullock, and across the street Detective Mulligan emerged from his place of concealment in the areaway of an untenanted house.

Handcuffs were slipped on the doorman's wrists, and he was left in charge of the Commissioner's chauffeur.

In the deserted hall of the speak-easy, the Commissioner held a final council of war. "Mulligan, you take care of the barman. I think he's harmless from what Inspector Bullock says, but you never can tell. Whatever happens, we don't want him to raise an alarm; I don't want any shooting if we can help it."

After a few more whispered instructions the little party walked into the bar, and Mulligan who was leading the way covered Joe, the bartender, with his revolver. A minute later the bartender was led away to join the doorman in the Commissioner's car.

When Mulligan returned, the five men, revolvers in hand, gathered about the dining-room door; through the partition could be heard sounds of revelry—the clinking of many glasses and loud bursts of laughter. Marinelli's wedding anniversary party was clearly a highly successful affair.

Mackay turned the doorknob and the detectives entered.

At a long, flower bedecked table that ran down the center of the room sat eighteen people of various genders and age. On either side of Marinelli, who occupied the far end of the table, were two wizened old women, so exactly alike in features and clothing that even the "pea in the pod" simile would be entirely inadequate to describe them.

Just behind Marinelli's chair, at a little table of their own, sat the Italian's six-year-old triplets and the three-year-old twins. Looking very subdued, and wearing stiffly-starched dresses and suits, the children stared at the detectives with questioning brown eyes.

The diners at the main table, equally astounded, regarded the detectives' entry with a little more excitement.

Chipo Marinelli half rose to his feet, and Maria screamed hysterically.

"Sit down," ordered the Commissioner, "and stick 'em up high—all of you!"

Thirty-six arms were raised simultaneously toward the ceiling. The three detectives searched the diners' clothing while Mackay and the Inspector stood guard.

"No gats," Dennis observed after a few minutes.

"Come over here, Marinelli," commanded Mackay, waving his revolver significantly. "And you, too, Mrs. Marinelli—your anniversary party's all over."

The two left their places and stood together in the middle of the room.

Mackay walked over to the head of the long table, and looked searchingly at each of the guests' faces.

"Know any of them?" he demanded.

Bullock shook his head. "No, sir," he replied. "But I think we'd better have a few words with that man." He pointed to a stocky individual, whose large, black, drooping whiskers and ruddy, fat cheeks gave him the appearance of a child at a fancy dress wearing a false mustache.

Mackay motioned the man to leave the table, then he turned to Maria Marinelli. "And last but not least—just so you won't be lonely in jail—we'll take your twin brother to keep you company."

He pointed to a young man who had been seated at Maria's right, "Come on you!" he ordered.

With a puzzled and frightened expression on his face, George Rivers, the Stock Exchange page, got up from his chair and joined the little group already under arrest.

18
THE END OF THE TRAIL

In a large, unused room at Headquarters the Commissioner and Inspector Bullock sat in triumphant state, surrounded by a buzzing swarm of inquisitive reporters.

So many questions had been asked simultaneously, that Mackay was finally forced to appoint Thorndyke of the *Times*, the oldest reporter present, to be the official interrogator for the press.

"To start with, Inspector Bullock," said Thorndyke, "will you tell us when you first suspected that Maria Marinelli was the murderer?"

"Well, boys, it was this way," replied Bullock expansively. He settled back comfortably into his chair and puffed at his cigar with an appearance of complete satisfaction. Like most of his ilk his affability to newspapermen usually waxed and waned in direct accord with the success or failure of his various investigations. Today he was in the very best of moods and was prepared to give the assembled newspapermen more than their fill of facts and figures.

"It was this way," he repeated. "The puzzling feature of the two poisonings on the Exchange was that we knew there were at least seven people who would benefit by Philip Torrent's death, but there didn't seem to be anyone who had cause to kill young Sandy Harrison. For a couple of days we used up valuable time in trying to find a man or woman who had reason to kill *both* these brokers. Naturally, we couldn't discover the connecting link between the two deaths because there simply wasn't any.

"Last night, as I lay in bed, I kept repeating to myself—'Why did the curare enter the systems of both men through a cut either on or near their ears? Over and over,' I demanded, 'why on the ear, why on the ear?' I said this so many times, as I tried to drop off to sleep, that the words turned into a silly little rhyme, and, suddenly, as though my subconscious mind had been working overtime, another line added itself automatically to the doggerel.

"'Why on the ear?
Why on the ear?
Because, ears hear!
Because, ears hear!'

"I leapt out of bed. Perhaps the poison had been placed on a telephone receiver? But if so, why was it that in Torrent's case the right ear had become infected while in Harrison's it was the left? The only possible answer to the question was, that Harrison might have been left-handed. I phoned Headquarters, and asked Inspector Martin to look at the photographs the Homicide Squad had taken of the two bodies. He told me Harrison's wrist watch was on his right, instead of his left, arm, and I was then almost positive as to the truth of my theory. To make doubly sure, I telephoned Harrison's office this morning, and his secretary informed me that my assumption was correct.

"This proved Harrison's death had been the result of an accident, since the curare had entered *his* body through the fingernail scratches which Lucy Laverne had given him the previous night. Although I didn't know which phone Sandy Harrison had used, I knew Torrent had been in booth number twelve in the Stock Exchange smoking room, and also in booth four at the 18 Broad Street entrance, for I had found, on the Exchange floor, two telephone slips notifying him he was wanted at those particular booths. Therefore, I cut off the receivers of these two telephones and had their bases analyzed at the Morgue office of the Chief Medical Examiner. On one of them there was found distinct traces of curare.

"Harrison's death having been proved an accident, we then concentrated on finding Torrent's murderer. Naturally, the killer must have had access to the Exchange. Now, there were three men, young Howard Torrent, Jack McDonald and Temple Hastings, who hated Philip Torrent and who were on the Floor at the time he was poisoned; but none of the three could have cut Torrent's ear; therefore, much against my will I had to admit that either these men were entirely innocent or that one of them had had an accomplice on the Exchange who aided him.

"Having been forced to widen the investigation, we decided to find out, if possible, whether any of the people under suspicion had ever been in Paraguay or Brazil—for these two countries are the only places where curare is produced. It appeared reasonable to assume that neither Lucy Laverne, Mary Torrent, Chipo Marinelli nor Howard Torrent had ever lived in either of these countries; but we soon learned that Jack McDonald spent a few days in Brazil only last year, while Temple Hastings had been for many years the owner of a large plantation in Paraguay. Therefore, both of these two men could easily have procured a supply of curare, and, adding to this the fact that Howard Torrent had studied at a medical school and was then presumably acquainted with the poison, we came back to precisely the place we started: the very men who couldn't possibly have committed the murders were the only ones who could have been familiar with curare.

"In the course of learning more about Paraguay, we consulted the *Encyclopaedia Britannica*, and waded through a mass of statistics about its population, geography, history and products. As I was glancing through this dry as dust information, I came upon a few lines telling about the founding and the early days of the country.

"Paraguay, like most of the South American nations, was originally settled by missionary priests who came over from Spain and Italy in the sixteenth and seventeenth centuries. The Encyclopaedia stated that the first Christian mission in Paraguay was established by Franciscan monks in the year 1542, but that they, due to the hardships of the life and the enmity of the Indians, were forced to return to Europe; whereafter, there remained no permanent settlement until 1605 when a band of Jesuits headed by three intrepid priests named Cataldino, Mazeta and Lorenzana finally succeeded in establishing a colony on a firm basis.

"The three names, Cataldino, Mazeta and Lorenzana, struck a responsive chord in my memory. Where and when had I heard of these men? I racked my brains and suddenly it all came back to me. These were the names of Marinelli's triplets.

"It was then obvious that there was some sort of link with Paraguay existing in the Marinelli family. It seemed unlikely that the connection could be on Chipo Marinelli's side, so I decided to learn more about Maria's background. At first I saw no way of finding out if she had Paraguayan blood, but finally I remembered that Marinelli had casually told me that today was his wedding anniversary.

"While questioning him this morning, I had noticed his dining-room was being elaborately decorated as if for a party, and, when I inquired the reason, he informed me he'd been married ten years ago at the City Hall, and was giving a dinner party that night in honor of the occasion."

"City Hall?" interjected the *City News* reporter. "How could a speak-easy proprietor get the mayor to marry him?"

The Commissioner smiled broadly and made an acid comment. "He couldn't in this administration, but it wouldn't have been a hard job to arrange—ten years ago."

After the laughter caused by Mackay's sally had died down, the Inspector continued. "As a matter of fact, what Marinelli meant was that he'd been married at the regular license bureau at the Municipal Building. You all probably know that in Italy and France the civil marriage ceremony must be performed in what they call their Town Hall. Since Marinelli was a comparatively recent arrival in America, it is easy to understand why he called our Municipal Building the City Hall."

The reporters solemnly wagged their heads in unison. For once their intense interest in a story was keeping their tongues discreetly quiet; they waited breathlessly for Bullock to resume his narrative.

"I, therefore, went to the Municipal Building and looked up the marriage records of April 4, 1925. I soon found what I desired. On that day Chipo Marinelli, aged 27, of Milan, Italy, was married to Maria Rivarola, aged 15, of Asuncion, Paraguay.

"I had now connected Maria with the country where curare was most used, but I still couldn't figure out how either she or Chipo could have gotten onto the Stock Exchange floor, and I probably never would have solved the case if I hadn't seen a story in the magazine section of the Sunday American.

"This article was entitled 'What Science Has Learned About Plural Births.' It told at great length the difference between fraternal and identical twins, went into details about the Canadian quintuplets, and pointed out that twins almost inevitably ran in certain families for generation after generation. Remembering that Maria Marinelli was not only the mother of twins but of triplets as well, I asked myself could it be possible that she, or Marinelli, had a twin brother employed in some capacity on the Stock Exchange. With this question in mind I visited the personnel department of the Exchange and searched through a list of their employees, hoping to find either the name Marinelli or Rivarola. Unfortunately there were no such names but I did find a George Rivers, and by consulting the exhaustive case-histories which the Exchange has tabulated concerning their employees, I learned that George Rivers had been born in Paraguay. It was then evident that he might be a brother of Maria who had anglicized his foreign-sounding name on his arrival in New York.

"Hardly daring to hope that my twin theory could be proved sound, I went back to the Floor and interviewed this young man. One glance was sufficient to assure me that he was unmistakably Maria Marinelli's twin brother. However, since I wasn't sure whether he'd been actually involved in the murder, I merely spoke to him for a moment giving no reason to suppose I was any more interested in him than in any other of his fellow pages. I didn't want to frighten him prematurely, if he were guilty, for I felt confident that he would be at his sister's anniversary party, at which time I intended to take him and the Marinellis into custody."

The Inspector paused for breath and looked keenly around the semicircle of listeners; then he rapped his knuckles on the side of a chair as if to emphasize his next words.

"The murder, of which crime the page boy was entirely innocent, was committed in this fashion."

The reporters leaned forward; impatient pencils were poised over bulging notebooks.

"On the evening of Monday, March 31st, Maria Marinelli invited her brother George to dinner, and, since he lived in the suburbs, it was arranged that he should stay the night. Before dinner, according to Chipo Marinelli, who has confessed his part in the crime, two drops of croton oil were mixed into George Rivers' butter."

"Croton oil?" demanded the *Tribune* man. "I never heard of that."

"Ask some of your friends on the tabs," advised Bullock. "They'll know. It's a sort of Mickey Finn—only ten times worse. After you've been given a drop or so, you aren't at all interested in going to work next day.

"But to continue—" he added. "The following morning, Maria took her sick brother's clothes, on the pretext of having them pressed, and, after trimming her already very closely cropped hair, she put on his clothing and departed for the Stock Exchange."

"But how—?" began Thorndyke.

"I know what you're going to say," interrupted Bullock. "You want to know how she knew the routine of the Exchange. Isn't that so? Well, it's simpler than it appears."

He reached into a pocket and drew out a little brown pamphlet.

"This," he said, reading aloud the inscription on the cover, "is called 'A Manual for Use by Employees of the Floor Department of the New York Stock Exchange.'" He tapped the booklet with a finger. "This manual, which is printed by the Exchange, is so complete in detail that even a person ignorant of the duties of a Stock Exchange page boy could easily get the hang of the ordinary rules and customs which govern them. For instance, it tells at what hour the pages are expected at work, to whom and how they report, where they sign their names on arrival, when to don their uniforms, how long they are allowed for lunch, at what hour they should leave the locker room and many other such items.

"This booklet, which was in George Rivers' pocket, had probably been seen by Maria on several previous occasions, and, since her brother had been employed by the Exchange for a number of years, she'd probably many times talked to him about the details of his duties. So far as she was concerned, she felt confident that even her brother's best friend would not discover her identity, for I have never seen two twins more strikingly similar in appearance.

"When Rivers realized on Tuesday morning that he was too sick to go to work, he asked his sister to telephone to the timekeeper at the Exchange and inform him he was unable to show up. Maria, we now know, told George Rivers she had done this, but, instead, wearing his clothes, she set off to take his place on the Floor. In her brother's suit was the key to his locker, and, as Maria had purposely gone to the Exchange rather early, she had no difficulty in donning her brother's uniform, before the dressing room became crowded.

"Her prearranged plan was to cut Torrent's ear with a phonograph needle, but, finding the red metal pencil, she inserted the needle and blacked the point with a match, thereby making a more formidable and less conspicuous weapon. The next step was to have Chipo call Torrent to the poisoned phone while she herself was at lunch. At two o'clock she telephoned her husband to inform him that she was about to put the curare on the receiver. To her consternation, she heard he'd been arrested on a liquor charge and taken away to jail. Under the circumstances she did the only thing possible to save their plan from failure. She went into a booth and spread the poison on the receiver; then, in the midst of the hectic trading in International Air-Conditioning, she scratched Torrent's ear. Afterwards, she went into a near-by booth and telephoned Torrent herself."

"Well, I'll be darned," remarked the reporter from the *Christian Science Monitor*. "She might even have been talking to him from the adjoining booth?"

"Quite possibly," agreed Bullock. "Anyhow, some time after Torrent had been called to the poisoned telephone, but not until after the unfortunate Harrison had used the same booth, she returned and wiped the curare off the base of the receiver, but, in doing so, she was so foolish as to leave a quantity of the poison in the diaphragm where I afterwards found it."

"That's plain enough," admitted Thorndyke. "But why did Marinelli telephone Torrent the first time, early in the morning? That call was not for the purpose of killing him since you found no poison on the receiver in the main Telephone Exchange."

"He says he wanted Torrent to go bail for him," explained the Inspector. "That may be true, but I think it's more likely he asked Torrent to reconsider his demand for the return of the seventy thousand dollars. When this request was refused, he went ahead with the murder."

"But how can you be sure young Rivers didn't purposely allow his sister to take his place?" demanded Thorndyke. "Why do you say he is absolutely innocent of any complicity in the murder?"

Bullock answered promptly. It was evident that he had considered every aspect of the case and was prepared for any questions the press might demand.

"His sister told me her brother was ignorant of her intentions, and I have also further proof that he was unaware of her presence on the Floor. To revert back to the subject of the little brown Exchange manual, on page 8 of that booklet one finds this regulation: 'Before an employee may return to active duty after absence due to illness, he must report directly to the medical department for examination and approval before he can enter the locker room or mingle with other employees.'

"Dr. Martin, the medical director, has informed me Rivers came for this examination on the morning after the murder, but since a boy who had not been absent on account of sickness would hardly report at the hospital, they naturally didn't inspect the timekeeper's record for the previous day, on which list Rivers had been marked as present."

"And the kidnapping of Lucy Laverne?" inquired one of the newspapermen.

"Chipo Marinelli's work. His uncle, whom we arrested at the restaurant, was the short, red-faced kidnapper described by Laverne. The uncle was also the fake postman who so neatly fooled Dennis and Hawley."

Bullock rose to his feet. "I think that's the whole story, gentlemen. If there's anything else you want to know, I'll be glad to tell you later. I've just remembered it's after ten o'clock and I haven't even had my lunch."

"Nor I," added the Commissioner. "Come on—let's go out and tear up the town. This is one night we ought to give ourselves a good party."

The reporters gathered up their hats and coats and began to move slowly toward the door. The man from the *Evening Post* lingered a little behind the others.

"Inspector Bullock," he said, "I certainly think you've handled this case wonderfully. Your story sounded just like a good detective novel."

Bullock turned on the man and looked him over from head to toe; then, calmly and unemotionally, he uttered a single word, "Nuts!"

The reporter has often wondered how such a simple remark could have made the Inspector so coldly furious.

Coachwhip Publications

CoachwhipBooks.com

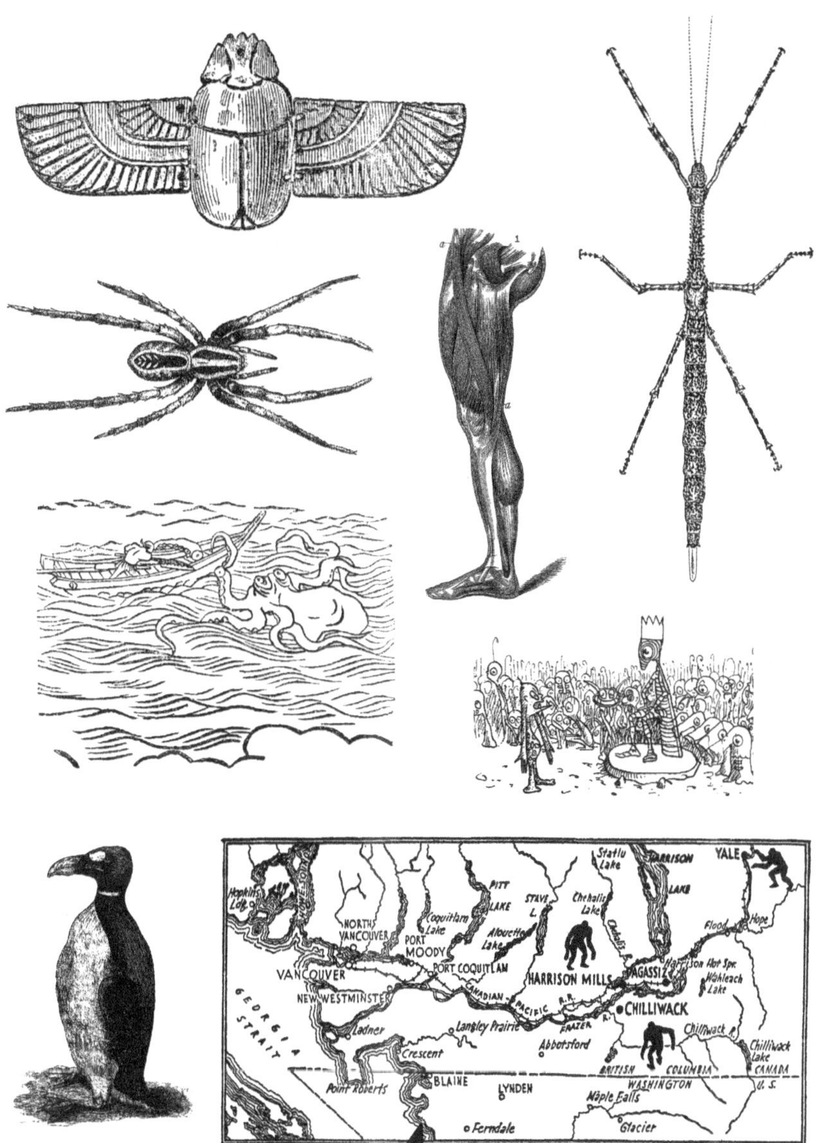

Coachwhip Publications

CoachwhipBooks.com

ISBN 978-1-61646-198-0

Coachwhip Publications

CoachwhipBooks.com

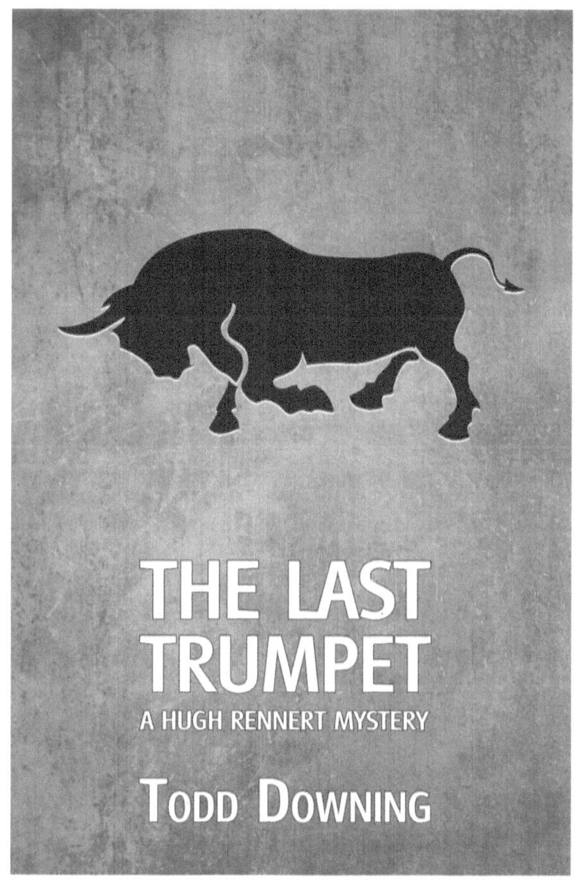

ISBN 978-1-61646-152-2

www.ingramcontent.com/pod-product-compliance
Lightning Source LLC
LaVergne TN
LVHW091147080826
845145LV00008B/2286
9781616462116